New Beginning

New Beginning

A Twiddle Series

SAMANTHA RAE

Library of Congress Control Number:		2010913553
ISBN:	Hardcover	978-1-4535-7538-3
	Softcover	978-1-4535-7537-6
	Ebook	978-1-4535-7539-0

This is a work of fiction. Names, characters, places and incidents either are the product of the author's imagination or are used fictitiously, and any resemblance to any actual persons, living or dead, events, or locales is entirely coincidental.

This book was printed in the United States of America.

To order additional copies of this book, contact:
Xlibris Corporation
1-888-795-4274
www.Xlibris.com
Orders@Xlibris.com
86055

CONTENTS

DEDICATIONS

I would like to dedicate this novel to my family and friends.
Without my family, I never would have been able
to get to this point of my life where I wanted to
write—thank you for always being there for me.
Without my friends, I would not have had the support
that I have outside of my family.

PREFACE

A single tear sprang from my eye as my back was slammed into a surrounding evergreen tree. I opened my eyes and saw death staring back at me.

I tried to scream. His hand, covering my mouth, muffled my cries. I could feel and smell the hot sweat streaming off his hand as it pressed hard against my lips.

I tried to escape and run. The tremendous weight on top of me was causing my entire body to go numb against the bark of the tree as it jabbed through my shirt.

Just a couple of minutes ago, I was sitting on the cold, dewy grass with my friends and boyfriend while watching movies at the outdoor theatre. Nothing was better than at that moment. I desperately wanted to get back to them.

I recalled everything that happened earlier that week to try to see why he would want to hurt me. My head was in so much pain from the beating against the tree, I couldn't think straight.

"I made a promise to her that I would help her out as best I could. You understand why I'm doing this then, right? I'm merely giving her what she desires. She wants you to stay out of her life forever." He was staring at me through dark blue eyes, and freshtears escaped from my burning eyes as he was explaining his actions.

I kept my focus on him as I saw his face change before me. His eyes transformed from dark blue to bright gold in an instant. His teeth grew wet, sharp, and pointy at the same time as his eyes changed color.

I forced a muffled scream once more, tapping into my will and energy as he lowered his head to my burning watery flesh.

CHAPTER 1

First Day

This wasn't one of those dreams where you know it's not real so you don't worry. No, I was having the type where everything seems real.

I was deep within a blooming forest, so much so that you couldn't see where the way out was or even the blue sky above the trees. I could feel the cold, wet morning dew coming off the blades of dark green grass and onto my bare feet. I could smell and hear the trickling water as it rushed down a nearby stream. But I wasn't here in the darkened forest alone.

Only a few feet away from me stood a tall dark muscular guy with light blue eyes like the afternoon sky; he stared right at me from the shadows of the surrounding maple and oak trees. I slowly opened my parched mouth to ask him what his name was, but I couldn't find my voice.

My dry throat started to burn. I couldn't draw enough air into my lungs to offer a single utterance. I was going to take a small step across the wet grass to be closer to him. Before I could move forward, I noticed something inching beside me from the corner of my eye. I turned to the right for a better look at what caught my attention, and I saw it was a large animal poised to strike. It looked like a giant brown grizzly bear, and it was strategically stalking the dark figure across from me.

The figure in the trees continued staring at me with fresh tears welling in his eyes when I saw the bear. The bear rose to its hind legs before it sprang and tackled the guy right in front of my very own eyes. I was frozen in place by petrifying fear and shock. My entire body ceased with numbing horror. I couldn't move an inch or extract my eyes from the bear as it brutally killed and consumed the unsuspecting man in front of me. I could discern the sound of bones being ripped from sinew and cracked. I could smell the blood as it was spilled from the victim's body.

After what felt like a lifetime to me, the bear finally stopped moving for a moment. Without any will to stop myself, I shifted my eyes to the remains of the guy who was previously very much alive. His detached limbs were strewn about, and the surrounding area was drenched in his bright red blood.

A low, deep snarl commenced deep within the bear's chest as he swung his head toward me; seeing it look at me jolted my complete attention back to what was happening before me. I was powerless to revert my eyes from the animal's big red orbs as the low, deep snarl was now growing into a full-blown growl from its chest.

The bear took a couple of steps away from the twitching remains of the body and dug its claws into the dirt as it loped toward me. I knew I should turn and try to run for my life as fast as I could, but I was paralyzed. The animal halted a few feet away. I could smell and see the fresh blood dripping from its sharp canines in its slightly open mouth. The animal leaned back as it bore its long nails into the grass, tearing up the dirt and leaving the ground beneath it bare.

I knew exactly what was going to happen to me next. The animal was going to attack with its claws and teeth. I was going to die. It was as simple as that. With a final helpless mental plea to my legs, though an unsuccessful one, the animal pulled his bloodstained lips back from his teeth before he lunged at my head. Once I saw the back legs leave the ground, adrenaline surged through my veins. Right away, I raised my arms to shield my face, but I wasn't quick enough before the bear made contact.

I gasped for air as my eyes widened in fear. I sat ramrod straight up in my bed instantly. *Just a dream, Britney, just a dream,* I kept mentally telling myself as I tried to slow down my breath. I left my navy blue curtain open the night before and now stared at hundreds of little white dust particles dancing in front of my face from the upcoming sunrise.

As my gasping breath and my racing heartbeat tried to get back to normal, I got up in my old light-gray sweatpants and my black-and-blue-striped T-shirt. After stretching a little, I slowly walked barefoot over to my desk. The night before, I had dug out my purple bag of toiletries, so I didn't have to worry about finding them this morning. Clutching the bag in my hands, I slowly went across the hall to the empty bathroom.

The only bathroom in our house had a counter along the right side of the wall with a mirror half the size over it. It had a silver bathtub/shower and a matching toilet near the corner. The walls were painted a light purple, and the floor was smooth and ice-cold on my feet with its black-and-white shining tiles.

With my heartbeat and breathing finally back to normal, I took another step closer to the mirror to see what my facial damage was for that morning. *I hope that I don't look as bad as I feel today.* No, of course not—I looked horribly worse.

My past-shoulder-length straight dark brown hair was cotton-ball puffy and all over the place in dripping spikes. *This will take hours of plain torture to brush through this disaster!* I tore my eyes away from my disastrous hair to see what makeup damage I'd have to worry about.

If I didn't look at my bright forest-green eyes, I would have never noticed that I was on the brink of crying. I wasn't really sniffling that much. My eyes were red and still full of tears while my high cheekbones were red with embarrassment. *I don't know why—I've always been the only one in the house during the mornings, and it was only a weird dream.* I ran my sleeveless arm across my eyes before the water in them could spill over and went to have a nice hot shower to get out the tension in my back.

A relaxed sigh echoed from my lips as I entered my new room. My room had a double bed in the middle of the back wall beside the only window. Beside my bed on the left was a little wooden end table with my black alarm clock and my dark red light on it.

My desk was along the wall opposite from my bed. My computer and a couple of my favourite books, which I wanted to get out right away, were on my desk along with everything that I thought that I would need for my first day of high school in this town. I couldn't see much of my fuzzy blue carpet floor with the boxes and boxes of clothes and other items all over the place in clusters.

I crossed over to one of the boxes with the words "Britney's Clothes" written on it, hopefully to find something perfect to wear for my first day. After I dumped the contents of two boxes on my bed, I found my favourite pair of low-cut dark jeans, my light blue T-shirt with a funky design, and my new black hoodie.

It's colder up here in Silver Stakes than it was back in LA. Last night, I slept with over five blankets to get somewhat warm. I had finally learned how to work the heater in the middle of the night.

With a final look at my clothes and makeup in the full-sized mirror in the hall, I grabbed my one-shoulder schoolbag. *I wish I could just stay in bed.* Knowing that I'd hate this place even more at the school, I went downstairs to the kitchen for some breakfast.

The kitchen had a long white counter along two walls with a sink and an espresso maker for my mom on it. There was a large white fridge at the end opposite of the window. In the middle of the room sat four wooden chairs around a table with a note on it. I walked over and read the note.

Britney,

Have fun at school, you'll make lots of new friends in no time. You'll have to tell me all about it later.

Love you lots.
Mom

P.S. I'm working late tonight to get everything together. Get some sleep and don't wait up.

I never really understood what my mom did as a living. All I know is that she is very independent at work—that, and her job pays well. The only downside to it was that it keeps her away for hours; I hardly ever see her.

My dad, however, used to work in a small section of the recording process. That's where I get my interest in music. I loved to talk to him about the music industry and the new talents, before my parents got divorced and I had to pick which one I wanted to live with. There was no choice for me to make.

It was extremely easier to live with my "never-around mom" than it was with my yelling drunk of a dad. *At least she leaves me little notes asking questions and still stays in touch with me.* My father never said anything to me since he randomly started drinking for a living, other than asking me for money.

At the time, I had a job as a waitress when he lost his job, and we didn't have any form of income from him. Once I could finally drive, he kept asking me to drive him downtown to a semi local bar so he could get drunk somewhere else. I also got calls from the bartender asking me to come and pick up my dad.

With my mom's newest note still held in my hand, I went over to the counter and wrote my thanks and love on it so she could see it if she stopped back here before she spent the night at work again. After finishing my bowl of cereal, I washed the dirty dishes, grabbed my bag, and left the house for my first day of high school in Silver Stakes.

•••

It only took me around fifteen minutes to get to the outside of the school. *I can't believe that they go to school here!* Okay, I knew that there weren't that many kids in Silver Stakes, but I never knew that they had a school this *big* for so few students. It was even bigger than the one I used to go to in LA. This school had what appeared to be two, maybe three, levels plus other smaller buildings around the school.

If my mom had mentioned that the school here was this big, I would have said, "Let's move there today," and not tried to hold it off as long as humanly possible. There were other cars in the parking lot, so I made my way in. There was an old rusted iron gate in between the ten-foot brick walls, but it was open wide, so I just drove on in.

I was making my way into the low-populated student parking lot when I noticed for the first time what the name of the building was. In dark crimson red letters, it faintly spelled the word "Twiddle," not SSH like it should from the name of the school I was given before I evened moved here.

I noticed this while driving up the dirt road that led into the parking lot. With my face going hot and red, I quickly turned around in my navy blue Pontiac Sunfire and headed down the main road looking for the proper building.

I hope that the owners didn't see me or that they have a camera set up near the gate. I didn't want to get in trouble right away. I tried to get my mind off it and tried to focus on finding the right building.

After driving down the road for about around another five minutes, I found another building that looked barely like a school in my standards. I looked at the name of the building and let out a breath of relief when it was the right building. It meant that I didn't have to drive around anymore. It also made me feel better that I made sure it was the right building before I started driving down the driveway.

This school was a lot smaller than the first building I drove into accidently. It was a one-level building, but it looked like it took a lot of property to have it on. There were only a few cars in the parking lot when I drove to it on the soft dirt road. It looked like an old school but with brand—or semi- brand-new things.

They had a Canadian flag waving around in the wind in front of the main doors. Their school letters were a bright red. *So the other building must have been an old school. But it doesn't look that much older other than the dark red letters. Wonder what's wrong with it. It would have made a perfect school.* I stepped out of my car with a sigh after I heard my feet crunch at the impact of the dirt on the ground.

Might as well get this over with so I can figure out what is up with that other building. I walked over to my trunk and popped it open to get my schoolbag. With my bag in hand, I took one last long breath of cold Canadian air by my car before turning toward the smaller school, and I started walking to the school's two main doors.

Once I was inside the school, I realized that it looked just like my old school, just a *lot* smaller. It had a weird smell of orange as I walked through the doors. The hallway floors were white tiles that shone before everyone walked on them. While I walked along the smooth floor, I heard my shoes squeak with every step I took.

All along the pearl-white walls were pictures of people, probably some of their old principals. We had one almost every new semester. Along one wall was a collage of several different large pictures painted on from top to bottom. I stopped just to look at all the different things involved in one picture.

I walked a little while down the hall before I found the main office. There was a bright trophy display case beside the office doors with old metals and plaques from past years. Each one had a picture of the team right above them. Some of them only had one person in the picture.

When I walked into the wooden office doors, I noticed the soft dark gray carpet first. I could see some darker dots all over if I looked hard enough. Looking up, I saw three completely organized wooden desks along the wall and one desk near the middle of the room facing the door.

All of the desks along the wall were empty, but behind the middle desk was a lady working away. She looked to be around thirty-five years old; she had curly red hair that went just below her ears. She had a straight nose that held her black-rimmed glasses on for her.

When I shut the door quietly behind me, trying not to scare her if she was deeply into what she was doing, she looked up with her small brown eyes and looked me over. "What can I help you with today, young lady? Have I seen you around before?"

I saw smoke swirling up from her desk, and when I walked closer to her desk, I could smell strawberries. Not long after that, I noticed that she was burning incense over a cigarette ash tray.

"Well, I doubt that you have. My name is Britney White, and I just moved here from LA and—" I was watching the smoke moving and dancing in the air when she cut me off.

"Oh, yes. My name is Mrs. Jaclyn, and I'm the main secretary here at SSH." She looked back at her desk and moved some papers around before looking back up at me. "I have your schedule right here along with a map of the school so you don't get lost in our many halls." She handed me the papers, and I saw that my name was written neatly on both papers along the top and bottom.

"Classes start in about twenty-five minutes, so I'll let you get going so you won't be late on your first day." Mrs. Jaclyn got up from her desk, placed a hand over my back, and walked me to the door while she talked. "Good luck, and welcome to SSH, and remember that I'm here to help you along, with all of the staff members around here."

By the end of her welcome speech, I ended up in a hall full of students walking around mostly in groups. Listening to them talking, laughing, and yelling around me, I looked at the sheet in my left hand at my new schedule for this semester. *Wonder what kinds of embarrassment in class they can put me through.* I'm always the kid that gets embarrassed the most during class, and everyone used to wait for it to happen. At least I had amazing friends that always had my back. A low semi-relaxed sigh left my lips when I saw two of my favourite subjects listed for me to take.

1st hour-room 210-English101-Mr.Colin
2nd hour-room 130-Drama200-Mrs.Wonderlich
3rd hour-Lunch
4th hour-room 301-Math101-Mr.Divident
5th hour-room 225-History200-Mr.Herbst
6th hour-room 400-Gym101-Ms.Gone

I would have preferred music instead of drama, but there were two problems. First, all the possible classes were completely full and had a lengthy waiting list for me even to be considered next for. Second, they only had instrumental and no guitar. I played other instruments, but I've always wanted the guitar class. It was that or nothing for me.

I took a quick look at the map to quickly study where I needed to go to get to my first class; this way, I wouldn't have to carry it around in my hand like a tourist. As I studied it, I realized that I had desperately wished that the first building was the actual school and not this little building. Then I would feel way more comfortable and relaxed about being here.

I had my one-shoulder-strap bag resting on my shoulder where it wasn't going over my chest. I usually wore it like this when I was going inside of it, and when I was putting my map in my bag, someone's shoulder slammed into mine. I spun around and stayed balanced, but they knocked my bag off of my shoulder. As it hit the floor, all of its contents spilled out of the bag, scattering on the floor.

Great, just my luck. Sigh. Kneeling down on the floor, I opened my bag up so I could shove everything back in. I was starting to gather my stuff together from the hall floor when another set of hands appeared and started to help me. *Or they're going to grab what useless stuff I have and run for it.* "Man, some people can't watch where they're going in the halls."

I looked up from the floor, and the first thing I saw was his big brown eyes staring back at me through his dirty-blond hair. "Hi, I'm Cole. Welcome to SSH, and don't worry, not everyone here is in such a hurry most of the time." He helped me put all of my things into my bag.

We slowly stood up by the office wall, and I struggled with my bag as I tried to cram everything back into it so it would close. I wasn't even paying any attention to see if I had everything off the floor. I wasn't really worrying about it at the moment.

Cole was still staring at me, probably waiting for me to say something back to him. *Why can't I speak when I need to the most? He must think that I'm stupid for not saying a single word to him yet.* I was about to say thanks for helping me with my stuff when this skinny bleach-blonde girl came over, didn't notice my existence, and pulled him away by the forearm. *Wonder what her problem is.*

"Come on, Cole, we can't be late again!" While she was saying this, she finally acted like she noticed me. It wasn't like I would have thought though—she gave me a deadly glare through her dark blue eyes. *And I thought they say that people in Canada are nice!*

Cole was still staring at me while he was being pulled by the arm quickly backward by the girl. *I hope he doesn't hit anyone while walking backward.* He looked like he was really balanced, but the girl pulling him looked a little clumsy just walking forward while she looked back at me. *Probably can't multitask either.*

"Yeah, okay, I'm coming." He said the words without looking away from me. "Hey! I'll see you around later. Maybe we even have a class or two together." While he said this, the girl gave me a "no way" glance over her shoulder as she just kept on pulling him behind her.

"Yeah, sure," was all I could get out of me as a response, and it wasn't even louder than a whisper. I wondered if he heard me;

this way, he wouldn't think that I can't talk at all. I felt my face getting hotter and hotter as I stood there looking after him. *Great. Just great. I didn't even get into class yet, and already, someone hates me, and the guy probably thinks I'm mental.*

CHAPTER 2

Good Morning

The English room was set up exactly the opposite of the one at my old school. They had tables instead of desks for everyone to sit at. The three walls surrounding the room were bare white except for a few random pictures of places around the world.

In the front of the class was a wall-sized chalkboard with what looked like lines from a book written on it. Right in front of the chalkboard was a big wooden desk with loose papers spread all over the place in small messy unorganized piles.

Mr. Colin was seated in a small black cushioned chair, writing on a student's test, at his large brown desk. He had hardly any hair except for some around his tiny ears. He looked like he was a little taller than me, but I'm not sure because he was sitting. Taking in a deep breath, I walked up to the desk and said, "Hi, I'm Britney White, and I—"

"Well, I've been expecting you. Welcome to English101. You can sit in the middle of table 4, between Stephanie Ozone and Leah Everwood. There're two of my best students in this class. If you have any questions about the material, ask them, and if for some reason they can't answer your questions, then come see me, and I will explain." He quickly looked up at me with his emerald eyes, and then he turned his eyes and pointed his red-tipped pen at a girl to come forward.

She was all in black except for her bright pink shoelaces, the white stripes on her knee high socks, and the dark pink covering her entire sleeves on her long-sleeved shirt. She had short curly light brown hair that bounced when she walked to the desk.

"Yes, Mr. Colin. What's going on?" Her voice was light and high. It reminded me of a baby bird.

"Yes. Take Ms. White back to your table and help her get settled in, and if she has any questions—"

"I'll answer them for her. Oh, and Leah won't be here for the next two weeks because she's on her family trip." Stephanie rocked on the balls of her feet.

"Thanks for reminding me. Now go and take her briefly through what we are doing today while I finish marking your tests from yesterday." With a final look at me, Mr. Colin lowered his head and went back to work, marking the remainder of the tests.

Stephanie started walking back to her table. As I followed her, I could feel the eyes of everyone in the room turned to me as I walked past them. My face was quickly growing in heat as I walked.

"Hi, I'm Stephanie, and you must be Britney. Don't worry about it, but in a school and town this small, everyone can't wait to see what you're like. People have been talking for weeks about you. Now that you're finally here, everyone wants to see if they were right." When I followed Stephanie back to the table, I realized that the lines were from the book *Diary of Anne Frank*.

"How far are you guys in the book?" We were finally at the seats, so I even saw the book on her side of the table.

"We're just starting it today. Here, I got you a copy. Mr. Colin told me that you were going to be sitting beside me. I can help you get started and caught up in this class." She gave me a really torn copy of the book, and she took her seat at the window.

"It would have been Leah. She always helps Mr. Colin. Seeing as she's not here for a while, she can't really help you. So it looks like you're stuck with me for a while." She looked over at me and gave me a wide smile. "Here, you can also borrow my notes so you won't be lost on anything we talk about for a while." She handed me a neat light-purple notebook that had her name maliciously written on it. I looked through and saw that it was halfway filled with notes. *Well I know what I'm doing for the next few nights.*

"Great, thanks. When do you want your book back?" I closed the book and looked at Stephanie, who was already reading Anne Frank. She stopped reading and looked at me with a growing smile.

"Well, seeing as you're new to the school, you will probably have a lot of work to catch up on. So—whenever you get done with it." She shrugged her shoulders and started reading again. "I don't mind if you take longer than a month—just remember to bring it every day so I can write down any notes. That way, I can keep all of my notes together and in order."

"Okay, thanks, and I'll try to remember that." *Hopefully, it won't take me more than a month to write all of the notes for all of these classes.*

I couldn't believe how nice she was to me. Usually, people would only lend you their notes for that night and they would expect that you got it all done, even if you were the new girl. That's how it was at my old school. We got a new girl in my grade before I left. Luckily, she was in some of my classes, so I looked at how she was treated in them so I would know what to expect. This is the complete opposite of what happened to her.

"So what do you have for the rest of the day? Maybe we have more than this class together." She sounded really hopeful about it, so I dug into my bag and handed her my schedule. As she looked at it, a grateful smile slowly expanded over her face.

It turned out that we were also in the same history and gym class together, and she was ecstatic when she found out that I had those classes with her. "You should come and have lunch with me and my friends. Of course, if you don't want to, that would be fine." I was shoving my schedule back into my bag when I heard her voice getting quieter after the bell rang. Everyone else was getting settled in their seats around us.

"Sure. Besides, if everyone is talking about me for weeks, then I bet all of them want to meet the new girl." At least I had someone to sit with at lunch. It means that I wouldn't look weird standing by myself, looking for a place to sit.

Not like that new girl back home—there was a rumour going around that she ended up eating lunch by herself in a bathroom stall. When we saw her after lunch, her makeup had been slightly smeared.

Before she could say another comment back to me, Mr. Colin cleared his throat; he then started the lecture about the book that we were going to read for the next two weeks. Then we took a couple of notes, and before I knew it, the hour was up and everyone was packing their stuff up and leaving the classroom.

After class, Stephanie showed me where my drama classroom was. When I got in the room, it took me a while to realize that we were in the gym. The only thing telling me that it was the gym was the basketball nets and the floor.

Everyone was surrounding the stage when Mrs. Wonderlich walked out onto center stage. She had blond hair that was pulled into a ponytail that went to her shoulders. During the entire class, we copied notes on how to use expression properly in a play. *This is why I love music the most—less notes and more doing things. Next year.* Near the end of the hour, I was starving, and I couldn't wait to see what their cafeteria looked like.

As I walked into the cafeteria, I was surprised by how big it was. The food was along the far wall with a long line formed by student and teachers. I saw Mr. Colin in line and was surprised that I was right about his height. I glanced around the room and noticed that there were easily over a dozen tables all over the place; there were five or more plastic chairs set up at each of them.

Right in front of me, I saw Stephanie waving her hand crazily in the air at me. So taking in a deep breath, I started my way to her table at the other end of the cafeteria. Even more people stopped and stared at me as I walked by them until I got to Stephanie's table.

Seated at the table there were two guys and another girl, along with Stephanie; they were already eating their lunches. When I came to the table, they all stopped eating and watched me for a moment.

"Hey, Britney. I saved you a seat." Stephanie pulled out a chair for me before she took her own seat. She took her eyes away from me to her friends. "Everyone, this is Britney White, we have first, fifth and sixth hour together." She beamed a very bright smile at me like I was saving her by being in the same classes as her. She looked from me to the other girl while she introduced her to me.

"Britney, this is Melanie Winchester . . ." She pointed to a black haired girl with brown eyes and glasses. Melanie looked at me and said hello like anyone would when you're introduced, so I said a friendly hello back to her, and she smiled.

She looked like she was really smart, but I could be wrong. Some people who look smart could be dumb, and people who look and act dumb could be really smart. It really depends on who they hang around with.

If she was really smart, hopefully, we would have math together because it's not my strongest subject. While I was making mental notes in my head, Stephanie continued with the introductions.

"This is Mat Yutzi . . ." She then pointed to a dark, curly-brown-haired guy. He looked like a really nice guy, but then most guys do. That Cole person seemed like a nice guy. You could tell that if a guy goes out of his way to help the new girl pick her stuff up in the hall that he's a nice guy.

When Stephanie said his name, he nodded at me and said hi and welcome. I glanced back at Melanie, and I could tell that she thought that Mat was nice; it was in the way she looked at him.

I'm not extremely good with relationships, but I'm sometimes good at telling if someone likes someone else. Only I'm not as good at telling if someone likes me, for some weird reason. Alanna always said that it was because I was always busy doing something that I never thought of a guy liking me like that. Jessica thinks it's because all the guys like playing against me, seeing as I give them a challenge. Seeing as I play against them constantly, she thinks that I don't really see them other than teammates.

"And last but not least, this is Sam Thompson." Stephanie pulled me out of my relationship daydream and back into the present. I looked at Sam and noticed that he had straight light brown hair that started to curl inward at his ears. It looked really cool in the bright light. He gave me a quick wave and went straight back to eating his pizza. *He must be even more starved than me.*

He also appeared to be athletic by the way his body looked, which could also be another reason that he was eating so much. He had another slice of pizza, an apple, chips, and a big cookie on his tray, along with some bottled water. *I wonder if he has gym before lunch. That would also explain it. I always get really hungry after gym if I have enough focus on it.*

"Hey, Britney, do you have a lunch with you? Because at this point the line will take forever to get through." Coming back again, I noticed that Mat said this while he nodded into the general direction of the line. After I followed his nod, I saw that he was right.

"Yea, I did bring one. I wasn't sure about the food here—even if it's good, I wouldn't know the price. Today, I thought I would play it safe and . . ." Searching through my bag, I realized that I must have forgotten to pick it up in the hall. "Oh. Shoot! Something must be against me today." *Hopefully who ever has my lunch will enjoy it.*

"What's wrong? Did you forget your lunch? If you did, then you can have some of mine. My mom always packs me way too much for me to eat anyways." Stephanie asked in a real nice voice while shoving some of her lunch across the table toward me.

"No, I didn't forget." I realized that I would finally have to tell someone about what happened outside the office, so I took a deep breath. It only looked like Stephanie and Melanie were the only ones interested in my story anyways; the guys were sill eating.

"While I was outside the office this morning, someone hit my shoulder. I would have seen them coming if I wasn't looking at my schedule. When my bag hit the floor, it was still partly open, and everything fell out. Then—" I started to say more, but my lunch suddenly landed on the table inches away from my crossed arms. Everyone around me, including the guys, had their mouths wide open while they stared over my head. I had no clue why they would be so shocked.

"As I was walking away, I saw that you forgot your lunch on the floor after the collision. I thought that I would give it to you when I saw you again." I looked up at him, meeting his brown eyes, and saw him give a very warm smile to me while he spoke. "Which would be at this moment." While he said this, he leaned forward a little, and his smile became slightly bigger. Behind me, I heard Stephanie drop her fork in her Caesar salad.

"Thanks, Cole. I really appreciate it, and thanks again for helping me gather my stuff up off the floor." I gave him a nice, sweet smile as I said this. He seemed to get even more enthusiastic about that.

"No problem. If we have any classes together, talk to me, and I'll help you get caught up in it if you want." He was staring right into my eyes, and I wondered what he saw in them. That, and I wondered if he saw me starting to blush.

"Sure, um, I'll keep that in mind." When I said this, I felt Stephanie poking at my back with her finger. I turned to her, unwilling to take my eyes away from Cole's, to ask her what was up; but Cole started talking again before I could ask.

"Well, I better let you guys eat. I'll see you later." When I turned to look at him again, he was already walking to a table on the other side of the room. When I looked at who was sitting there, I saw a bunch of guys and girls talking to each other except for one. It was the same girl from the hall, who was glaring at me through slit eyelids. *Wow. If looks could possibly kill!*

"Okay, so how in the world does Cole Parson know you? He doesn't have any classes really near you in the morning." Stephanie said while, thankfully, pulling me out of her deadly glare.

"Well, I was getting to that part." I turned toward Stephanie and the others while ignoring the glare I was getting from behind me. "See, while I was picking my stuff up, he came by and helped me." I grabbed my bun from the bag, ripped it, and ate it. I was so glad that I had some food in me, especially if I had gym later today.

"Wow! He looked like he likes you, so you're going to have to be careful." When Stephanie said this, the members of the entire group were nodding their heads together in agreement. And I realized that they were talking about the blonde girl who was probably imagining slowly torturing me right now.

"Why? Does it have to do with the blonde girl a couple of tables over?" I had to know for sure. Maybe they could tell me more about her. I might as well know who I should watch for if I still can't convince Mom to move back to LA soon.

"Yeah, that's Rebekah Morency." Mat leaned forward on the table, whispering to me while the others were eating their lunches. Everyone looked like they weren't listening, but they probably were. Mat continued, "She is the most popular girl here. Everyone always talks about her—"

"Until someone heard about you and told everyone that you were moving up into town. People were talking about what they thought you and your mom were going to be like for weeks." After Sam said this, he gave me a quick look over as to see if they were close to what I looked like. Then he went back to eating his already-half-eaten apple.

Mat gave Sam a dirty look for interrupting him in his explanation. "So as you can guess, the popular people never like it when someone that they don't know takes the spotlight from them. Plus everyone is still talking about you, so you'll probably be in the spotlight—" Mat kept on saying with a calculating look on his face while he calculated how long I would have to be in the center of attention around here. I didn't want any of it, so I just spoke my mind. *Maybe they could help me give it back to Rebekah and away from me, for good.*

Mat was still calculating, so I interrupted him to stop him from trying to figure it out. "She can have it. I don't want to stand out here right now." I realized that Mat might be mad at me for interrupting him like how Sam did, but he didn't look mad at me at all; he looked more amused that I'd stopped him.

"It's way too late now," Melanie said with a look of concern on her face. "She's seen you talking to Cole, and no girl alive talks to Cole. Especially like that. And apparently, she saw you talking to him just now."

"He's the one that's talking to me, not the other way around." I looked at Melanie, but she shook her head.

"It doesn't matter. If he talks to you, you're just supposed to walk away or tell him something *before* she sees you." As Melanie was explaining this, I remembered the warning look in the hall that she gave me and now the deadly look that I was getting.

"Well, that explains the look in the hall—" I started to say before some water hit me in the face, so I had to stop talking to wipe it from my face. *Gross!*

"She saw you talking to him in the hall!" Stephanie was the one that spit the water into my face, and she was now close to screaming at me too.

"Yeah, she gave me this weird look. So I take it she saw him helping me with my stuff because while he was talking to me, she came along and pulled him away." When I explained this, everyone stopped what they were doing and stared at me. Even Sam stopped eating his chips and stared at me while I explained all of this to them. After I finished talking, the guys shrugged their shoulders and went back to eating their lunches.

"Stephanie, question. You said that Britney doesn't have any morning classes with him. So what afternoon classes does she have with him?" As Melanie asked, I realized that I really wanted to know too. *Hopefully, Rebekah won't be in any of my classes. I doubt that in a school this small, I would be that lucky though. Well, at least, I could probably beat her up. She looks like the type that won't carry anything, anywhere.*

"She has fourth and sixth hour with him. I'm not sure if Rebekah has the same fourth, but she does have the same sixth I hope that she doesn't have the same fourth as him."

"She doesn't." Mat sounded a little upset at that fact, and I didn't know why. Isn't it a good thing that she doesn't have the same fourth as me? "She had the same as me sadly." Wow. I hope that he doesn't have to sit beside her—that would be torture for anyone.

"It's good that she doesn't have the same fourth as you, Britney. I'm really sorry for you, Mat. I can see why you wouldn't say anything to us about it." I looked over to Mat while Stephanie said this, and he just nodded to her.

"At least I'll be there during sixth hour to have your back if she tries anything on you during gym." Her expression suddenly got all cheerful like someone just gave her a giant present that she's always wanted. It was weird how someone can change their expression so quickly.

"In gym, we're starting badminton. You're lucky because you just missed dodgeball, and it's harder than anything else that we play the entire year." Stephanie rubbed her left arm as if she was rubbing a tender bruise. "Do you want to want to be partners? Then maybe if she sees you staying away from Cole, she won't be as mad at you as she is at this moment."

I thought about it for a second and realized that I didn't want to get Rebekah even more wrathful at me. And I would like to be partners with Stephanie for the first time. "Sure, then no one else will know how bad I am with playing sports, at least." I said with a big smile on my face.

I'm actually really good at physical activities, even dodgeball. But they don't need to know that yet, but I'm sure that Stephanie will find out during gym, unless I can control how much energy I put into playing.

In LA, I was the only girl in the class to put up a challenge for the guys. Tarah was good too; we always were the more full contact out of the girls, but the guys hardly stopped us.

During the rest of the hour, the five of us laughed and talked the entire time until we had to leave for class.

CHAPTER 3

Long Afternoon

"Okay, here's your lucky math class. I want to know every little thing that happens in there. No matter how small it is. This is the only class that you and Cole are somewhat alone in." Stephanie was kind enough to help me locate where my math room was. We were outside the door talking before she had to leave to go to her class so she wouldn't be late. She was starting to become my best friend here. Out of everything else that's happened so far today, I was surprised and glad that she was so nice to me since the beginning.

"Thanks, and if anything interesting happens this hour, then you'll be the first person I tell it to," I said as Stephanie started to leave. She turned around and gave me a little nod before walking even faster so she wouldn't be late to her class. I turned away from her, took a deep breath, and went into the classroom. *Relax; it's just another class in this totally small school. Nothing to be nervous about.*

And it was just another class. The classroom looked almost exactly like the English room, except for the fact that the board had some long complicated math equations, not lines from a book. Also along the walls were posters of math rules and little funky math cartoons that looked bizarre.

I walked up to the board where Mr. Divident was writing even more questions out of the textbook and told him who I was. He was expecting me. Just like everyone else in this entire school.

Mr. Divident had really short black hair; he looked to be about six feet tall, but he had thick black shoes on, so who knows? He gave me a seat near the window of a table near the back and a brand new textbook for the rest of the school year. Finally, he told me that the students seated beside and around me could help me if I get lost or stuck on anything that we talked about today. *Teachers are completely dependent on the other students to help them out with their job of helping the students get caught up.*

With my new textbook in hand, I went and sat at the table that I was assigned, taking my seat near the window. I was looking in the textbook at the page that Mr. Divident was writing on the board, trying to figure it out, when I heard his voice coming beside me.

"See, I told you that we would have a class together." I looked up from the math page, which I didn't understand how to figure out, and saw him seated beside me with a huge friendly grin on his face. *Rebekah will hate me—oh, well. Maybe he can help me with the stupid math. Hopefully, I can talk and be myself around him. I hope I don't sound as stupid like I usually do—might as well give it a try.*

"Yeah. Well, I guess that in a school this small, everyone has a class together." I decided to smile at him even though I hate how small this school is. Schools should not be this small—it's not normal. And his smile just got bigger after I said this. *Wonder if he can tell that I hated that fact.*

"That's how it is here. What do you have for the rest of the day? Maybe I can walk you to your next class." He sounded like he really wanted to have another class with me, so I had to tell him. Even though I already knew what classes he had from what Stephanie said during lunch. *Weird how she knew exactly what classes he has.*

"I have history in room 200 and then gym in room 400." I tried my best to sound enthusiastic about it, but I hate history. That was my worse subject for years. I was so bad at it that the teacher even ended up hating me because I hated history. That made the subject even worse. At least I had gym to look forward to during history, even though Stephanie said that Rebekah was in it.

Without him even knowing about my past in history, he kept on talking. "Great! I know that you'll enjoy gym at least. See, today, we're starting—"

"Badminton. Yeah, Stephanie is already trying to get me excited about it." I wondered afterward if he was the type of person that would get mad at anyone if they cut him off, but he looked even happier that I did interrupt him. I showed him that I wasn't in the complete dark about things that were happening around here.

"That's good. We don't play sports the usual way around here. You'll see what I'm talking about for yourself today." Cole took a deep breath, and before I could say anything about it, he started talking again; his smile faded a little as he talked. "So I guess you're going to be Stephanie's partner for today then, right?" He sounded a little upset about the fact that I might already have a partner for today.

He doesn't even really know me, and he's getting disappointed that I might already have a partner for gym. Wow. Now I wish I was nicer to the new girl, but then I would have to leave soon after knowing her better. Maybe she should have moved up here instead—she would have been treated nicer here. I wonder why Mom even picked to move up here. She hates small towns and the cold just as much as me.

While thinking this, I thought that I wouldn't put that much energy into gym today. *I don't need to be that enthusiastic about gym yet*. I also didn't want people to get the impression that I'm good at every sport. Last year, the coach was bothering me every day to join the teams, but I never did.

After thinking about me not trying my hardest in gym, I thought of the perfect thing to say to Cole. "Then gym should be interesting for me and will probably be really entertaining for you along with everyone else, if you play by different rules." Cole laughed a real quiet laugh, trying not to bring any more attention to us, and shook his head slowly at me. He couldn't say anything back to me after he stopped laughing because the bell rang, then right after the bell stopped, Mr. Divident cleared his throat and started the class.

We were finished with today's note about halfway through class, so we were to work on today's assigned homework for the rest of the hour. When everyone went into little conversations, Cole turned to talk to me again.

"Here, you can borrow my notes and give them back to me whenever you're done with them." He handed me his black notebook that looked like it was easily filled halfway with notes. *Great, even more work for tonight. On top of everything else! There has to be lots of notes for history too. Great. At least there can't be that much or any notes for gym. By the sounds of it, they play a lot of games. Good, just a couple more minutes, then I get to leave this class entirely behind me.*

"Um, thanks." I took the notebook from him. Apparently, I made a face when I took it that he thought was funny because he tried to hide his laugh as a cough, unsuccessfully. He then looked straight at me while he tried to explain how his notebook works.

"Don't worry, okay? The notes aren't that long, and in the beginning, I wrote the homework in it to." He opened the book to show me what he was talking about, and I saw how neat he could write. "But then I thought that I should separate them. I also write big on the notes. See, so you don't have to copy any of the stuff that looks like this unless you want to. They can be examples if you still don't get the note." We both looked up from the page and stared into each other's eyes again.

"Ah, Mr. Parson, I'm glad that you're helping your new classmate Ms. White get up to speed in this class." Mr. Divident was standing on the other side of the table, staring at us with his hazel eyes. *I wonder how long he's been standing there.*

"No problem, Mr. Divident. I'm happy to help out as much as I can." He looked away from me and gave Mr. Divident a smile. I noticed that everyone in the class other than us was at the door, waiting for the bell to ring. *They must hate math as much as me.* "I know how stressful it can be to teach a class and make sure that everyone gets what you're teaching."

"That's good. Maybe you could help her get ready for the unit test this Friday." Mr. Divident was looking right at me, so I just nodded. *Great, I'm not even here a week, and I already have to take a unit test.* "If you want, I can give you extra points on anything you want depending on how much she gets right on the test." He turned his gaze back to me. "This test won't go to your final grade at all—this will just help me know how much you learned in your last school."

"No problem." Cole turned toward me, meting my eyes again, and smiled. "I'd love to help out another classmate study."

"Good to hear." The bell finally rang, and everyone left the classroom in a rush. Mr. Divident started walking away from us, and we started to pack up quickly; but when Mr. Divident was about halfway back to his desk, he stopped and turned around to face us again. "Oh, Ms. White . . . Welcome and good luck in the rest of your classes." From the corner of my eye, I saw that Mr. Divident gave me a small smile, so I gave one back to him.

"Thanks." I was saying this to Mr. Divident, but I couldn't take my eyes away from Cole's. After what seemed like hours to me, we both got up from the table, with our bags in hand, and left the room together. *Hopefully, Rebekah won't be waiting outside the room and see us walking out of class together.*

"Do you know where your history class is?" Cole was leading the way out, and after he passed the door, he slowed down and turned to look at me. He sounded like he didn't want to leave me right now, and I didn't exactly want him to leave either. But I also didn't want to risk Rebekah seeing me with him again today. *She is probably going to kill me already from before.*

With a small sigh, I said, "Yeah, I do. Stephanie told me where to go, and she also said that she would wait for me outside the door." After I looked around—checking if Rebekah was around watching us—I looked him in the eyes again, and he looked in mine. He didn't look too upset about the fact that I already knew where it was. Probably from the fact that this isn't that big of a school, so you can't really get lost here. *I really hate this school in more ways than one.*

"Okay, then. I'll see you later in gym." He gave me another warm smile and walked off in the opposite direction. It took me a moment to find and use my legs again.

Gym is going to be real interesting today for several, maybe everyone, in the class.

During the entire fifth hour, Stephanie was asking me question after question on what happened in math class. I told her everything that happened, and we agreed that he really liked me. I was waiting for her outside the change room, seeing as I changed quickly so I could talk to Ms. Gone.

I already had my black shorts on underneath my jeans, so I was quicker than normal. I really wanted gym here. The only problem was that I didn't have the right color shirt on for today.

When Cole walked out of the guys change room, he didn't come over, but he did smile and wave at me. *How long can he smile for? He's got to be getting tired of smiling at me.*

"Yup, he's definitely into you." Stephanie's voice came out of nowhere, so like typical me, I jumped. Out of the corner of my eye, I saw that Cole thought that it was funny. "Sorry, I didn't mean to scare you." Her face dropped, and she looked like she was concerned that she scared me.

"Don't worry about it. You just surprised me, and I also scare easily when I'm deep in thought sometimes." I shrugged, and Stephanie looked slightly better.

"Okay, class. Get with a partner, and let's start the games. We're going to do the same mini tournament that we did on Friday." Ms. Gone's voice was loud and clear before she walked out of the storage room with two buckets. "Grab a birdie and a racquet, then claim a random court and start playing."

On our way to the buckets, Stephanie was explaining the game to me. "Okay, so you score a point the same way as before, but it's different before and after each one." She handed me a racquet, and we started for a court as she continued to explain.

"If the point scored is questioned by someone on the other team, or they think that it was different, you can choose to have little *challenges* between each point to decide who gets it." We were by ourselves at the far court by the doors; she stopped walking and was watching me take this in.

"Challenges like what?" While I said this, Stephanie's blue eyes got huge. I could only guess why.

"Like balancing on one foot for the longest or playing rock-paper-scissors." I turned around, and sure enough, it was Cole standing behind me, smiling. *Nope, he's definitely not tired of smiling.* "Do you mind if we play you two? We promise that we'll go easy for your first time." We were staring at each other for a while, and I couldn't find my voice; thankfully, Stephanie answered him.

"Um. Sure." Cole and his smaller black-haired friend went to the other side of the court. Stephanie turned her back toward them so they wouldn't hear her. "No matter what, you might as well go for him. She's never going to lighten up on you, especially if she sees the way he's looking at you." Stephanie nodded her head toward Rebekah. I followed her gaze and saw that she saw me talking to him.

She gave me a look that said that she was going to murder me if I talked to him again. "I don't think I've ever seen him smile so much in his entire life." Stephanie saved me from Rebekah's look, but she gave me a look of happiness mixed with concern instead.

"Okay, I'll be extremely careful around both of them from now on. For now though, let's make the guys regret saying that they'll go easy." I gave Stephanie a sweet smile to make her relax. "They don't know how well I play sports."

"Let's get them." We gave each other a high five before we started the game.

Stephanie and I just barely beat the guys when we had to stop. "Wow. Britney, you're better at this than you let on." Cole was saying this when we did the customary handshake after the game. He had a warm, firm grip, and it felt like he didn't want to let go of my hand. I didn't want him to either, but he eventually did. We then continued on to the next court to continue with the matches.

We were almost done the playing games for today. We were placed against the other team that had as many wins as us. It came down to the four highest winning pairs left, and we were one of them.

"The two teams that are playing for the champion spot of the day are: Stephanie,-Britney and Rebekah-Emma. The first team to get to three points by the time the period is over will be the winners."

As we walked over to the court, I saw Rebekah's eyes stare right through me. *Great, she'll murder me for looking and talking to Cole. What a nice way to finish the day.*

"Relax. She can't kill you while people are watching—too many witnesses. Personally, I think you can easily take her." I looked over to see Stephanie's sincere smile as she walked beside me.

"Well, hopefully, I can. Otherwise, she will definitely kill me. Wait—if I beat her, then she'll kill me for that in the change room."

Stephanie was going to say more, but the whistle blew, and all the games around us erupted at the same time again.

Rebekah won the coin toss, so she had the first serve. She served the birdie to me, and I returned it back to her. This went on for several hits; after a while, I spiked the birdie, and she couldn't get to it in time.

"What did you just do?" Stephanie's voice was still smooth, seeing as her and Rebekah's partner weren't really playing.

"Don't tell me that you guys never learned how to spike yet." My breath was coming fast and hard, but I still managed to get the sentence out perfectly clear in one breath.

"No, we've never learned that. We just learned how to serve and return. Coach always likes to play the games instead of talking about them, except for the first day." Right then, I saw some hope spring to her eyes. "Can you teach me? Then maybe I can help you more during the game." She started to jump up and down with excitement.

"Sure, no problem. I'll teach you when I have more energy to actually talk." I crossed the court and got ready to serve the birdie back to Rebekah.

When I served the birdie, we were back to our one-on-one game. After a few moments, several people started to come to the courtsides to watch our game. We were only at 1-1, but apparently, several of the teams were completely done with their final game. I even saw the coach watching us intently as she ignored the other games that were still in session.

My rhythm was slightly interrupted when I saw Cole by Rebekah's court with a confident smile on his face. That little distraction gave another point to Rebekah. *Get it together, girl. You can beat her.*

Halfway through our final game, we caught a few minutes of break time when Emma hit the birdie too far off the court. I took advantage of it and tried to catch my breath again. We were about to start the game again when Coach blew the whistle.

"Fewminute break for everyone still playing so we can see everyone's current standings so far." Relieved for the longer break, I let my hand slide down farther on the racquet. It wasn't long before Stephanie just took it from my hand and placed her untouched water bottle in it.

"You're doing really well. I don't think I've ever seen people play like this." She tuned to look at Rebekah. "I don't think she's ever played like this before. She usually does nothing. I turned to stare at Rebekah who was also getting a drink, although she was sitting down.

"Don't sit down, walk it off, and stay standing." I crossed under the net over to her side of the court, but when she saw me coming closer, she just stared at me.

"What do you know?" She was still seated on the floor when everyone went over to see the standings. Well, everyone except for us four and Cole. He was starting to walk toward me.

"I know for a fact that you have to stay up and moving after a workout like that. Especially if you're not used to it. Unless you want to feel horrible for the next few hours after you get up." I held out my hand to help her up, but she just stayed there.

"I don't need any help from you." She started to stand up by herself, but she ended up falling backward halfway up. Thankfully for her, no one was paying much attention at that moment.

"Come on, Rebekah, you know she wouldn't do anything to hurt you, and I'm pretty sure that I've heard that too." Cole was standing beside me with his hand extended out to her. She took his hand in an instant.

"Well, all you had to do was say so." She never looked at me while she continued. "And I guess I should thank you for telling me about it instead of using it for your advantage." She held on to Cole for dear life as she talked. Looking like she would fall if she let go of him.

Instead of looking at her though, Cole was looking at me with the word *sorry* plainly spread throughout his eyes. And I knew why.

"Come on girls, let's see who is first today." Coach's voice boomed over all the little conversations that were going on. Coach had her arms folded over her chest watching us.

"I'm ready whenever you are, Rebekah." I ignored Cole while I walked back over to my side of the court. I needed to focus on the game at hand and not on personal stuff.

"I really hate her. You should have let her sit there and not help her." Stephanie whispered while we walked to our spots. She only wanted me to hear her obviously.

"Well, I'm not like that, and it should be a fair game." I looked over and saw her shaking her head at me in disapproval. "I'll teach you how to spike, and then you can kick her butt yourself."

"Well, when you put it like that." She stopped shaking her head and looked right at me. "Teach me right away."

"I will, but—" The whistle interrupted me, and we all looked at the coach. Coach looked ticked that we didn't start yet. We resumed the game right away.

Again, the game mostly consisted of me and Rebekah hitting the birdie back and forth. We were at match point when I decided to change who was playing.

After I slammed the birdie to the far back side of the court, I turned to Stephanie, "Your turn."

She looked confused as I grabbed her arm to put her in my spot. She instantly understood what I was doing and tried to back away.

"I won't be able to hit it far." She held her racquet just below her chin. It shook slightly as she felt some pressure.

"That's why I've already set it up for you, and if by a weird chance you miss, I'll get it again." I backed away a little just as Rebekah got to the airborne birdie and hit it back. The birdie went flying away from me and toward Stephanie.

She hit the birdie, and it just barely went over the net. Emma was standing in the far left corner staying out of the way when Rebekah yelled at her to get it.

Just as Emma started to run to get to the birdie, it bounced off the ground before she was halfway there.

Coach walked over to us and took our racquets from us. "Time to pack all the sports equipment up—get the nets out of the way as best as possible. Then hit the showers for today." Stephanie and I got several congratulations from other people, but not a single word was said to Rebekah after the game.

It was after my really short shower that I realized that I forgot to pack some deodorant. "I always forget the simple stuff."

"You can use my deodorant. That way, next time he talks to you, you won't smell that bad." Stephanie handed me her deodorant in the change room, and I was really glad. I really did put a lot of effort in the game today, even though I wasn't planning on it. "Did you know that you had gym, or was it just a guess?"

"I always have some—" I couldn't finish my sentence because I was interrupted again, but not by Stephanie.

"Don't even bother with Cole." I looked behind Stephanie and saw Rebekah giving me a hateful stare while she talked. "He's only being nice to you because you're new here, and he doesn't want to be mean to you on the first week."

Then a smile easily broke over her face as she looked me over. "He also likes girls that don't smell like sweat, and apparently, you go all out in sports. No big surprise there. You didn't even bring deodorant." She started to walk away, and I realized that she thought that I was scared of her.

"Well, it looked like he was enjoying the competition for a change, and apparently, you don't go all out with anything other than shopping, probably. I mean, who sits down right after playing a game? Anybody that works out knows what not to do after." Rebekah was frozen in place, with her back to me.

"This isn't over." She stood there for another moment before walking toward her little group of friends. Stephanie then hurried to dry off and get changed, then she pulled me out of there by my arm.

"I can't believe that you told her off. No one has ever done that to her since second grade. She's going to kill you, and everyone, except for some people, is going to hate you." Stephanie looked like she didn't know whether to be excited or terrified about me telling Rebekah off. Her eyes were huge, but she wasn't jumping up and down anymore.

"Hey, at least she knows that she can't scare me into doing anything she wants me to do." I looked over Stephanie's shoulder, and I saw Cole walking over toward us.

"Britney, I'm glad I caught you before you left." As he walked over, Stephanie gave a "go for it" look. "I was wondering if you would want to get together tonight sometime. We can study for the math test together then." He had little drops of water coming out of his hair and onto his face. He looked really cute.

"Um, actually, I already have plans." Stephanie gave me a confused look, and I realized that I needed to explain more. "Well,

I have to start copying the thousands of notes, and I also have to unpack some of the many boxes before my mom gets home . . . if she gets home."

"If you want, I can come over and help you out," Stephanie asked in such a nice voice I didn't want to be mean and say no. She probably just wanted to get to know me better. I could understand that, but tonight wasn't going to be the best.

"It won't be that much fun. There's lots of stuff to unpack and—"

"No problem. Just say when you want me over." Stephanie looked so excited about coming over and seeing where I was staying, but she probably knew where. She started to bounce on the balls of her feet again.

"*Us* over." Cole corrected Stephanie while giving us both a sweet smile. "Just say what time is okay with you, and I can pick up Stephanie along with some really good take-out food before I come over." Stephanie started nodding her head like a bobblehead, so I had to agree. It would seem wrong to disagree with them being so excited to come.

"Well, my mom won't be home until late probably, so whenever works for me." Cole's smile grew even bigger as I agreed to him coming over. Right as I was saying this, Rebekah walked out of the change room and gave me another deadly look. *At least she knows she can't scare me into doing what she wants.*

"I'm ready whenever you are, Cole." Rebekah came and put her arm through his while he just rolled his eyes. We both saw him do that, but Rebekah didn't.

"Okay, just give me a minute." He looked at Rebekah without any expression for a moment before turning back to us. "How about I take Rebekah home, get the food, and pick you up?" He looked at Stephanie before continuing his plan. "And be at your place in half an hour." He then looked at me, and a smile reappeared on his wet face.

"Okay, sounds good." Stephanie and I both agreed at the same time, and his smile got even bigger while Rebekah gave us both a deadly glare when we agreed to this. Then without saying anything, she started pulling Cole away by the arm.

He didn't stop looking at me until she pulled him around the corner.

"You know, she's going to kill me along with you now." When I turned to her, I saw her shrug her shoulders. She didn't seem concerned anymore.

"Oh, well, maybe Cole will protect us for the night." Stephanie and I walked out of school together, laughing about different ways Rebekah was going to kill us.

CHAPTER 4

A Night to Remember

I arrived home a little after 4:30 p.m., so I had a few minutes to spare before Stephanie and Cole showed up to help me unpack some of the thousands of boxes that populated the house. After I realized that I didn't have to do anything major to tidy up because there wasn't anything out yet to tidy up, I tossed my schoolbag on the long black couch and went into the kitchen to get a snack. With a granola bar in hand, I saw a new note from my mom in the middle of the table.

> *Britney, hope you had a great day at school today. Can't wait to hear all about what you did during the day. I have to work late tonight so I probably won't be home until the early morning. I placed some money on the counter so you can order a pizza or something for supper seeing as we hardly have anything to eat. I'll get groceries later tomorrow. Keep the money if you don't want any take out, and if you do buy something than keep the change. You can use it for lunch tomorrow if you want.*

Knock, knock. I was so into the note that I jumped slightly as I came out of it, but I knew that it would be Stephanie and Cole at the door. I walked over to answer the door while I read the rest of the note.

> *Don't worry about unpacking anything of mine in my room; I'll take care of it when I get home later. Mom. Ps I love you.*

I opened the door and saw Stephanie in the doorway, jumping up and down with excitement. "Hey, Britney, we're here to help you unpack." Stephanie was the one at the door while Cole was at the back of his red truck getting out the food for us to eat later tonight.

"And I hope that you don't mind, but I sort of told Cole what to get you, seeing as he forgot to ask you. Apparently, he looked in the phone book for your number. But he couldn't find it, so he was hoping that I would know what you would want." She then put up her hands as if to surrender to me for talking to Cole, which I didn't get because I'm not like Rebekah who hates everyone who talks to him.

"During the entire ride here, we talked about you. He really likes you." She winked at me just when Cole got to the door, and we both started to giggle.

"Hey, I don't know what's so funny right now. But I got the food, so let's get started." As the giggling became scarce for the moment, I stepped aside to let them in, and both of their mouths fell open in shock when they saw all the boxes that populated my house. "Do you have enough boxes, or is there more hiding?" Cole turned to me and smiled like he had been all day.

"These boxes are only filled with stuff for the living room. There are about the same amount of boxes in each room." I looked at Stephanie, and she still had her mouth open, so I told her how she had put this on herself. "Just remember that you both volunteered for this, and I told you that there was a lot of work to be done around here. My mom pretty much packed everything that we owned in the house. Left nothing for my dad."

I carefully took the bags of food from Cole and went to put it on the kitchen counter for us later tonight when we get hungry. Then I wrote a small note for my mom on a separate sheet of paper, saying that I made friends and how school was today.

"Um, where's your mom at tonight, Britney? I thought that she would be here helping out with unpacking the boxes or something." I glanced up from the note and saw Stephanie standing across the table from me with a worried look on her face. In the background, I could clearly hear Cole tearing open one of the thousands of boxes in the living room.

"She's out tonight, working. I hardly ever see her around because she works during the day mostly, but we write notes for each other, so we still stay in touch with each other." I held up the note to show Stephanie. "She won't be back until the early morning apparently." Then I remembered the money on the counter.

"Hey, how much did the food cost? I want to pay Cole back for buying food for me." I could at least pay Cole back for the food, then I could say that I bought take-out and give my mom the change back, even if she told me to keep it. *I need to find a job soon. Maybe they have a video store that needs some help.*

"Um, I'm not entirely sure. I told Cole what to get you before he picked me up." She giggled quietly so only I could hear. "He got a hold of my cell number after he couldn't find any of yours." I had to giggle with her. After knowing her for so long, he finally talks to her, and it's only because of me. Wow, high school, all right.

"Okay. Hey, maybe he'll keep it and call you more seeing as he has it now. And he won't have to look it up in the phone book for any future calls." I grabbed the twenty from the counter and went to find Cole in the living room while Stephanie looked more closely at the letter. After a moment, she started to add some stuff on the bottom for my mom. *Well, at least Mom can tell that I'm not making up the fact that I made friends again.*

Cole was standing on the far side of the room, placing some movies on the shelf by the TV. When I got to the table, he turned around. I turned my gaze away from him, and I unfolded the money in my hand.

"Here, this is for you." I stretched my arm out, and he started to shake his head. *Maybe he thinks that I'm paying him for helping me. I better explain.* I looked down again, and I explained the best that I could. "My mom gave me some money to pay for food tonight, and seeing as you brought the food, I'm giving it to you." *At least I could actually say something to him, even though I didn't look at him at all while talking. I need talking help!*

"Don't worry about it." I looked up, and he was going through the box, getting more movies to put up. He stopped and came toward me. "Consider it part of your welcome present." He was staring straight at me, and we were standing so close now that

I had to look up to see him smiling at me. I could feel my face growing hot as I slowly understood what he was saying.

"Did you say 'part'? How many parts are there?" I only softly whispered the questions, but he heard me perfectly clear.

"Yes, I said 'part,' and I'm still working on it," he whispered back to me, and for a moment, I forgot that Stephanie was in the next room and that she could easily walk in and see us like this. "I'll let you know what the other parts of the welcome present are as soon as I figure them out."

"How many parts are you planning for exactly?" We were still whispering to each other, and after I spoke, I could hear Stephanie walking around the kitchen. *Man, I hope she doesn't see us like this. But then she did say that he really likes me, so would this surprise her?* I mentally shook my head, trying to forget that I wanted to continue with this conversation.

How the heck do I tell him and everyone that I hate presents? I can't even tell my mom! But then she's not around when I get them. I shook myself mentally again, and Cole continued like I never stopped listening to him.

"There are a few ideas that I have thought about, actually." He paused and looked over to see if Stephanie was coming. I couldn't help but look with him. When I did look, I caught Stephanie skipping to the other side of the counter with the note.

Her back was toward us as she continued to write on the note. I could see several different colours of pens in her hand. I looked back at Cole, and he was talking before he was turning his head back to me. "But I'm going to spread them out, so you'll have to wait for a while to get them all."

I then heard Stephanie put the pens away in the drawer and apparently so did Cole. He then took a slow step away from me and chuckled. "So what do you need to unpack right away other than your movies?"

"Um, well, I have to unpack my clothes so I don't have to empty out boxes just for one outfit. But we can start here. At least we don't have to do my mom's room." Stephanie walked in then, and she looked like she loved to leave my mom a note. Even though she never met my mom and probably never will. *I wonder how much she heard of our conversation.*

"We can do your clothes, and Cole could probably unpack some more things down here. Unless he wants to help with unpacking your clothes?" Stephanie started walking toward the stairs as she watched us.

"No, that's okay," I answered for him before he could even open his mouth to reply. "I'm pretty sure that my room isn't the worst anyways. Most of my stuff isn't even here yet." I walked over to another box and opened it to examine what was inside. "I never really knew how much movies we had in our old house. I think we filled three boxes just with DVDs to bring." *Rambling again, have to work on that.*

"I got the movies taken care of, if you two are going to do clothes. I wouldn't want to mess anything up in there anyways." He walked over to me and started pulling out the movies. "Besides, after we get done, we might have time for a movie or two. This way, I know exactly what good movies you already have."

We ended up leaving Cole downstairs to deal with the living room boxes as we went straight to my room to unpack. *At least, this way, I don't have to worry about saying anything stupid with him in the room*. He also won't be going through my clothes. Now that would be weird.

Stephanie's mouth fell open again as we stepped into my room. There weren't as many boxes as everywhere else, but there was a ton of them. I crossed the room and started to unpack some boxes. Stephanie did the same. I looked over to see which box she decided to start with first. I was surprised to see her in my guitar box.

"Where do you want these books?" I knew that she didn't really look at them as picks and loose papers fell out of the bound book pages. I quickly made my way over to her and grabbed the books before even more stuff fell from them.

"What did I do?" Stephanie looked completely unaware of the stuff falling from the books. When I took them, she seemed upset, like I didn't trust her to help me unpack.

"Nothing, it's just that everything is falling out of the books. I mark my favourite songs by placing a pick or whatever's around me at the time in them." Stephanie held the books more carefully now, so I started to gather the picks and papers that fell to the floor. "It's weird, but I have way too many picks around." When

I stood up, Stephanie was flipping through the books, careful not to lose any more of my bookmark picks.

"You have a guitar? When did you get it?" I placed the picks and music sheets on the dresser and started to unpack some more books.

"I got it when I was about twelve, and I've been playing it ever since. I love it." Stephanie was looking around the room, and I knew that she wanted to see it. "It's not here. I couldn't bring everything with me. We didn't have that much room in the truck and trailer." I walked over to the dresser and placed some of the books in a pile.

"My mom insisted that I leave my guitar there so I would focus on getting caught up in school. She sent for it and my other stuff afterward, so I should be getting it and the rest of my things Saturday or Sunday at the latest."

"You'll have to play something for me and Cole when you get it." We returned to unpacking some more boxes as we talked about possible songs for me to play. She was getting more and more excited as she listed songs that I could play.

We were done unpacking everything we could by 7:30 p.m. Cole was done in the living room before we were done my room somehow and started to get the food warmed up and ready for us. While we ate, Stephanie informed Cole of my guitar, and he was almost as excited as Stephanie to hear some songs that I could play.

"What kind is it?" Cole was watching me as he ate some of his fries.

"It's a Polished Gloss Blue TB1-LU acoustic guitar." Stephanie stopped eating mid-bite, and Cole didn't pick up another fry. They didn't know much about guitars apparently. I tried to make it easier for them. "It's a really good acoustic guitar. I'll show you when I finally get it." That was pretty much the last time we talked about the type of guitar I had.

After we were all done with the food, we decided to watch a movie, seeing as they didn't have to leave yet. We decided to watch *Wanted* and leave the schoolwork until later. I was seated in the middle of the black couch, so when Stephanie eventually fell asleep halfway through the movie, her head hit and rested on my shoulder.

We were almost done with the movie when Cole said, "Do you want another pop? I can get it for you, seeing as you're now a pillow." Cole leaned in front of me and grabbed my empty can from the table before I could answer.

"Thanks. Only I think that there's only one left." I was whispering so I wouldn't wake Stephanie up from her nap.

"Then you can have mine." He turned and looked at me. My face would have gone red again, but when he looked at me, I saw a light from a car pulling in going across his back.

"What car just pulled in?" I nodded to the window while I really hoped that it wasn't Rebekah coming over to kill me for talking to Cole earlier. I reached for the volume and turned it down a little so I could actually hear him. Cole got up from the couch with the empty pop can in his hand and walked over to the window to see who just pulled in the driveway.

"It looks like a black Pontiac Sunfire." He was still looking out the window, but I saw his eyebrows move closer together as he tried to figure out who it was. "I don't know anybody in or near the town with that type of car." As he said this, I went through my head all the people with that car, but only one kept on coming to my mind. *It can't be!*

"It might be my mom, but it's too early for her to be coming home." After I said this, I heard the front door lightly locked into place, so I tried to get Stephanie off of me nicely so I could see if it was really her. I just put Stephanie's head down on the actual pillow, when I heard a faintly familiar voice.

"Hey, baby. I know I'm home early, but it felt wrong to leave you here all alone with everything still in boxes." We both walked over to each other and hugged one another, ignoring the audience. *I don't think my mom even sees that I have people from school here.*

Still in the embrace, she whispered in my ear, "Baby, do you know whose truck that is outside in our driveway?" With the hug over, Stephanie almost woke up but didn't, and Cole came over to us with his hand out to introduce himself. My mom's eyes almost went out of their sockets when she saw him. *I knew she didn't notice either of them!*

"Hello, Mrs. White, I'm Cole Parson." He shook my mom's hand, and she pulled herself together by the time he continued. "I can move my truck for you if you'd like. Stephanie"—he paused, and with his free hand, he pointed at my sleeping friend on the couch, and my mom looked at me, pleased that I made friends already—"and I were just helping Britney unpack all of the boxes."

"I can see that." My mom dropped his hand and gave a quick look around the room. She looked very pleased and surprised by the fact that there wasn't a single box in sight. "How much did you three unpack?" She didn't look at me when she said this; instead, she was looking at Cole.

I hope she doesn't have any unspoken rules about having a guy over without her here. But then she never is around to even notice that I'm here. The only thing that pulled me out of my mental rant was Cole answering my mom. I shook myself mentally so no one would notice that I was thinking to myself again.

"We've unpacked everything except for the boxes in your room, Mrs. White." Cole didn't even look at my mom; instead, he just looked at me while he talked.

"Please, call me Susan." She then looked away from Cole and toward me. "Unpacking all of those boxes must have taken hours to do. I hope that Britney didn't make you do too much or made you feel that you had to help her out." My mom gave me a *"using your new friends on the first day"* mixed with *"they must be good people to be friends with"* look. I could feel the heat starting to rise in my cheeks.

I suddenly felt the need to defend myself so my mom wouldn't think that I was using people because she's never around anymore. "They offered to come and help, so don't blame me." I saw Cole walk over to the couch to wake Stephanie up softly from her evening nap.

"That's true. Britney tried to warn us, but we wouldn't believe her. Anyways, I better get going before my parents start to worry." Letting out a sigh, he bent over and picked Stephanie up into his arms. "And I'll take Stephanie home on my way." He walked to the door with her in his arms. "Thanks for having us over." My mom walked over and held the door open for him so he wouldn't have to try to open it.

"No problem, and come over anytime. My job requires me to be away from home during the day, so I won't be around much to keep Britney company when she's home." My mom's voice revealed to me that she liked that Cole came to help me out with unpacking and that she would like to see him around more when she can. *I shouldn't get a whole lecture about having him over then.*

"I'm pretty sure that Stephanie will be over more than me." He gave a quick glance at me before turning to explain to my mom. "I'm on most of the sports teams at school, and they mostly practice after school, but I'll be sure to visit soon." He looked away from my mom and at me again before he left. "Hey, you should try out for a couple of teams. Tryouts are over, but I bet that seeing as you just got here, they'll let you try out anyways."

I considered this before I answered. "I would, but I should probably try getting caught up with everything in class first. That, and I don't really do school teams." I looked over to my mom, and she just looked confused that I would be good enough to even consider being on a team. She doesn't really know a lot about my life, seeing as she's always away working.

"Oh, well, maybe you'll change your mind later." I looked back at Cole, and he winked at me. "Anyways, Stephanie's just getting heavier. So I'll see you tomorrow, Britney." While he said this, he smiled at my mom, and then he gave me another wink. I felt my face getting really hot again. *I hope my mom didn't just see that or the one before. I might be getting "the guy" speech if she did.*

He turned around and carried Stephanie off. When he got the door opened, he put her carefully into the front seat of his truck. He gave a final quick wave to us before he got in the driver's side and turned the truck on. Before I knew it, they were driving away into the night.

After a couple of seconds of staring after them, I shut the door and locked it before I turned around and got another warm, welcoming embrace from my mom. During the next couple of hours of the night, my mom and I talked about what happened in school and what happened at home while she was gone.

She asked a lot of questions about Cole and Stephanie, and from what I told her, she liked that I made good friends on my first day. When I was climbing the stairs, I thought I heard her say something else. It sounded like she said, "It was a good choice to move up here." I shook my head and went to bed.

That night, after everything that happened, I ended up going to sleep at about 11:30 p.m., and my mom ended up going to bed at 11:00 p.m. I ended up going to bed later because I still had to do my homework. I only did the homework for my first classes of the day. I could finish the other stuff during lunch tomorrow.

CHAPTER 5

First Sighting

The next morning, I ended up getting ready for school a lot quicker than what I usually do. After a few moments of sitting at the table, staring at the digital clock, I decided that I would go to school early. When I got there, I would sit in my car with the heat on full blast and continue writing out the notes from all of my classes this semester.

Lucky for me, they got a hold of my schedule from LA before I even got here. The only problem is that they didn't have the same classes that I was having, so they just substituted some in what they thought were close to them. They thought that would make up for all of it. *I want to know how they think that drama is like music.*

While I was almost to my car, I decided that I would have my music blaring while taking my time driving to school. I had lots of time to spare. I was singing along with a favourite song while bobbing my head to the rhythm of the music when I saw something black move in a large blooming maple tree that hung over the top of a brick wall, from the corner of my eye.

I quickly pulled over onto the wet dark green grass and quickly got out of the car to check it out. I half jogged over to the huge maple tree and looked up into the tree to see what or who was up there.

"Hello, is anyone up there?" *I swear I saw something move in that tree.* I took another step closer. *I wonder who or what is up there.*

Just as I thought of this, several leaves fell from the tree and landed on my head. I got a glimpse of a long dark human figure as they jumped from the tree over to the other side of the wall.

"Hey, I just wanted to talk to you!" I quickly ran to the old rusted iron gate; as I got close to it, my shoes slid on the grass, and I lost my balance. I reflectively reached out for the bars of the gate to help me from landing on my butt. *Need shoes with more grip.* After a moment, I regained my balance, and I tried to open the gate.

After a minute of steady pulling on the gate, I saw that it had a digital lock on the side. Quickly thinking of a way to get in, I looked in between the thick bars to see if I could find who just jumped over the wall and away from me. *They won't be able to get out this way. Not unless they know the combination for the lock.*

I glanced around the dark green yard trying to see if they were all right after they jumped that. It was about a ten-foot drop down to the ground. While I looked around trees, benches, and other things in the yard, my eye was brought abruptly to the building in the direct center of the fresh yard.

It was the same big building that I thought was my new school and tried to get into yesterday. *I thought it was an empty building? Looks like I have some questions to ask Stephanie today that desperately need some answers.*

Giving up on finding the jumper right now, I let loose my grip on the bars and slowly headed back to my car. I didn't want to slip again. An arctic breeze spread and filled within my jacket as I walked back. I quickly closed my jacket by wrapping my arms around my chest. Within several steps of my car, I could hear my music through the doors and glass.

When I opened the door, the music grew even louder. After I closed the door, I turned down the music so I could think clearly for a moment. As I turned the music down, I cranked the heat up as high as it would go.

I just sat in my seat, just thinking. *I didn't know that it was locked.* I sat there with my hands grasping the wheel for several minutes before I started my way to school again. I had to pull over every so often just to think.

I finally pulled into the school, but there wasn't enough time to sit and copy any one of my notes. I got into my seat in English just as the bell rang for everyone to stand to the playing of "O Canada" and to listen to the announcements. All through the morning announcements and the English lecture, Stephanie and I talked about last night through notes.

In the notes, we talked about what we were going to do later that week; we were also trying to figure out how many parts that Cole would create, what they're going to be, and when Cole would surprise me with them. The incident this morning was completely cleared from my mind.

It wasn't until the last twenty minutes of lunch when I remembered to ask them about what the Twiddle building was. I had the perfect timing. Everyone was starting to pack their stuff away. "Okay, I have a question for you guys to answer."

Everyone went quiet and was staring at me, waiting for me to ask my question for them. Well, everyone was except for Sam; he was enjoying finishing his bag of chips way too much to even look up until he was done eating everything he had or if he got full. That apparently never happens, so I ignored him and continued to ask my question.

"Okay, well, I was wondering what that Twiddle building was used for." I looked around, and everyone was looking at each other, so I continued. "When I was driving here this morning, I saw someone jump from the tree over the wall just to get in there."

Everyone's eyes widened in shock the moment I mentioned the fact that I saw someone at the building. Sam even stopped eating his chips and was staring at me. I knew that it must be wrong to see someone jump over the wall to get in. Everyone was in so much shock from what I said that they just sat there staring at me for a while.

"You saw someone go in there! When exactly did you see that? What did they look like?" Sam was the first to speak after a couple of long moments of silence. Some uneaten chips fell out of his mouth as he spoke. He was so excited to learn more about this. *Definitely unusual to see someone there.*

"It was this morning. I was driving here to copy some of my notes in my car before class. As I drove by the building, I saw something move in the maple tree, so I pulled over to see what or who was in it. I was underneath the tree when the person jumped over the wall into the yard. I didn't see them that good to give a description, but I tried to follow them-"

"You didn't!" Stephanie was almost yelling. So I, along with Melanie, patted her shoulder to remind her that we were still in a crowded cafeteria with lots of people who could easily overhear what we were talking about. Stephanie closed her eyes and took a couple of deep breaths before she continued. "Britney, did you actually go in there past the gate?"

"No, I tried the gate, but it was locked. Then I looked in through the bars, but I didn't even see any sign of the person after they jumped over." Then curiosity really hit me. "Why? What is that place?"

Everyone looked a little more relieved from my answer, so Melanie and I stopped patting Stephanie. I looked around the table at everyone waiting for my answers. I knew that everything was back to normal for the moment because Sam went back to eating his chips while we talked.

"No one around town really knows what that building is used for." Mat paused for a second to see if anyone could hear us. "Some people say that if you're caught trespassing on the property, the owners will hunt you down and take you away somewhere so they can do experiments on you." Mat, along with everyone else, looked like they were going to be deeply upset if I said that I went in there. *I can't tell them that I've already been in there on my first day now!*

"One day, I saw one of my neighbour's nephews walk into the yard when I was in grade nine. Two giant middle-aged people came out of the building and forced him inside. I never saw that kid again."

"I thought he moved." Sam perked up a little.

"That's just what *they* want you to think while he was their prisoner. For all I know, that kid is six feet under now." Mat looked right at me. "Some people say that when you can go in there, that means it's your time to die."

"Mat doesn't mean to scare you Britney, but you can't go in there, not even past the gate." Melanie gave Mat a stern look for telling me the story. "No one knows what will happen to you if you do go in for sure. If you ever go in past the gate, though, you have to make sure that no one sees you in there."

Melanie looked back at me. "Just stay away, okay? We don't want anything upsetting to happen to the only girl alive in this whole town who tells Rebekah off now." There was a little smile touching her lips when she said the last part.

"Yeah, and I think that Cole will be completely heartbroken if anything bad happens to you." Stephanie put one of her hands on my shoulder to get my attention away from Mat. I looked at her, and she was smiling and completely perky again.

"Anyways, we all better get going to class, especially you, Britney." Everyone else started to finish packing up their finished lunches, laughing like nothing was wrong, and then Stephanie stopped and looked around. "Hey, it looks like Britney might have a date for Saturday."

"Saturday? What's going on Saturday?" Frozen at the words Stephanie just said, I looked around and, everyone was smiling like crazy at me. "Is anyone going to tell me?" Just then everyone looked down at their things, except for Stephanie who was still looking at me.

"Hey." Recognizing whose voice it was, I turned around. And sure enough, I was right. It was a smiling Cole standing right behind me. *Maybe his face is stuck like that for now, especially if he hardly ever smiled before.* "I was wondering if I could walk you to class." He looked at me for a moment, then he looked right at Stephanie. "If that's all right, if I steal her for the last couple of min—"

"Yeah, of course you can." Stephanie was back to her almost yelling but not quiet voice, and Cole's smile grew again. I looked over at Stephanie with wide eyes for how quickly she said this, and she just shrugged her shoulders at me in return.

"Thanks. Well, if you're ready to go." He locked eyes with me as he held out a hand for mine. I grabbed my bag after a moment of looking into his eyes.

"I'm ready." I turned away from his eyes and toward Stephanie's glistening, wide eyes. "I'll see you in history." She gave me a quick nod in agreement, not looking away from Cole, so I got up and gathered my things together before I headed to class with Cole. When we were outside of the cafeteria doors,

Cole took my hand to hold it. He had a nice warm touch, so I didn't argue.

"I hope that I didn't interrupt you all in a middle of a conversation. If I did, I didn't mean to, and I'm sorry." There wasn't even a hint of a smile on his face, so I took him very seriously. It was weird seeing him so upset about something that was perfectly fine with everyone. It was also weird to see him without a smile. *I wonder if this was what he was like before.*

"No, you didn't interrupt. They were just about to tell me what the main thing that's going on, on Saturday." I looked up at him and was glad to see a little smile that was tempted to spread on his face at any moment.

"It's a movie marathon. The school puts one on every other Saturday for everyone in and around the town. They usually have themes. I think the theme this time is adventure movies." The classroom was in sight, and Cole started to walk even slower. With my hand entwined in his, I ended up slowing down too. "You should go. I think you'll really like it. But then you probably saw them all."

"I haven't seen that many adventure movies. Are you sure it's adventure though? I don't want to go if it's actually chick flicks instead." He nodded, and I debated for a couple of steps. "Okay, I'll go, if I can find someone to go with. Where is it?" We've stopped walking in front of the door, and he turned to look at me.

"It's just on the outskirts of town. If you want, I can pick you up and drive you home later. I can also pick up your friend Stephanie. I'm sure she'll want to be there too."

I was completely overwhelmed by the fact that he hadn't been smiling at me for a while that I didn't even notice that I'd agreed to go with him until a huge smile broke out on his face again and he was back to his perky self again.

"How about seven thirty?" We then slowly started walking into the classroom. "You should probably ask Stephanie if that works for her, so how about you answer me during gym. And just think about it as another one of the parts." While walking into the classroom, almost everyone noticed that we were coming in together. *Great, someone is bound to tell Rebekah, and then she'll try to kill me in gym today again.*

I ignored everyone watching us coming in and continued my conversation with him. "Okay, I will." By then we reached our seats. I sat in my chair and prepared myself to pay attention to the hour-long lecture about quadratic equations so I could attempt to do them.

CHAPTER 6

Questions and Answers

During the entire history class, I never had a single chance to talk to Stephanie about anything until after class. For some reason, we didn't say anything about Cole until we were on our way out of the change room. "Okay, so tell me *everything*! What did you talk to him about? Did he ask you out? Did—"

I knew that she was never going to stop asking questions, so I had to interrupt her. Besides, it looked like she was going to pee her pants if I didn't tell her soon. "Well, first, he held my hand from the cafeteria to the classroom."

"How was it? From his handshake yesterday, it felt like he has a nice, warm, and strong touch." By the end, Stephanie's eyes were away from me and toward the wall as she imagined his hand entwined with hers. She also started to sway slightly from one side to another, like she was getting close to passing out.

"Hello, Earth to Stephanie! Do you want to hear the rest of it, or do you just want to daydream for the entire hour?" After I said this, Stephanie shook her head and gave me a stern look.

"What happened next? Don't leave out anything." Then as I predicted, she started jumping up and down on the balls of her feet.

"Okay, I'll tell you everything, but I have to start at the end because he needs to talk to me in here. Okay?" I gave a look toward the guys' change room, but Cole wasn't out yet.

"Yeah, okay." She wouldn't stop jumping, so I had to put my hands on her shoulders to hold her still.

"Okay, well, he told me about the movie marathon that's happening this Saturday." Instead of jumping up and down, she just nodded her head like crazy. "He then told me that I had to go to it, seeing as this is the first one that I'm here for. He also said that he was going to make this one of the parts. He asked me if he could give me a ride there, but there was a catch."

"What! What was it?" Stephanie was back to jumping against my hands as I continued.

"He told me what time he could pick me up, and then he asked me if you wanted to come too." When I said the last part, Stephanie instantly stopped jumping and looked completely shocked.

Just then we were instructed to grab a birdie and a racquet and then find a spot on the wall to practice our hits. I looked around and met Cole's eyes on the other side of the gym. He was being pulled backward by Rebekah again as he smiled and waved his racquet at me.

"Wait, he asked if I wanted to come with you?" I looked away from Cole to see Stephanie grab my arm and pull me toward the wall. I only took a couple of steps before she stopped pulling me.

"Yeah, he said that I might want you there for my first time. Then he told me to first ask if you wanted to come, then he said that he'll talk to me in gym. Which is happening right now." Stephanie and I were too busy talking to each other that we didn't realize that everyone was getting into partners until Cole and his friend came over right to us.

"So ready to kick some butt, partner?" Cole was staring straight at me when he said this, so I had no idea that he was referring to me. He always stared at me while he was talking to someone else.

"Sure." I said, a little shaky. The only reason I knew that he was actually talking to me was the fact that after he said this, he raised a dark brown eyebrow at me. So I guessed that he was talking to me.

While Stephanie and Cole's friend Max Salters walked to the other end of the court, I couldn't help but look around. Apparently, from what I could see, we were told to get into guy-girl teams and start playing for probably the rest of the hour. As I continued to look around, I met a fairly familiar deadly glare. From, of course, Rebekah.

For some reason though, when I met it, she lightened up and smiled at me. I could tell that she wasn't used to it because she quickly looked away, and the smile stopped completely when she started yelling at her partner for letting the birdie hit the floor on their side. *Poor guy! He probably had no one left to choose from.*

"So did Stephanie say whether or not she wants to come to the marathon with us? Or is it just you and me?" I turned my attention away from the poor guy and back to Cole. He was smiling a small smile at me as we walked to our sides of the court.

"Well, I only had time to tell her about it before you two came over, so she hasn't said yes or no yet." I looked over to see if Cole was upset about her not deciding yet, but he still had a smile on his face.

"Will you answer a question for me?" We were staring at each other, so all I had to do was nod, and he continued. "If Stephanie says no, will you still go with me?" When I opened my mouth to answer him, we got the go-ahead from coach, and all of the games started in unison.

Stephanie served to me, and I returned the birdie back to her. I wasn't going to go all out against her. None of us were really trying to beat the other. It went back and forth like this several times between the four of us before I answered his question through hits.

"Yes, I'll still go with you." I looked over to Cole when he spiked the birdie over the net, earning us another point. He grinned as he scored the point. *He's going to have facial damage if he keeps this up. No one can smile this much.*

"Really? You're not just saying this—you actually mean it?" When we crossed sides, I looked into his eyes while I answered.

"Yeah, I really mean it." There was a little sparkle in his eyes after I said this, then I had a question of my own to ask him. Before I could, he started talking again.

"Good. Then it's a date." He wasn't looking at me when I turned to him, but I did see a smile on him while he served underhanded to Stephanie.

Her eyes were huge like bug eyes, and her mouth, open so wide that you thought it would hit the ground. She quickly recovered as she hit the birdie over to me, probably to help me thaw after that. *Date! Why would I want my best friend there on a date with me?*

I saved the birdie, and now, I was fully focused on the game. I couldn't ask my question in front of Stephanie. *What if it was something bad? I would have to ask him after the games when everyone would be talking more.* But as I thought about waiting for everyone to get louder, they did. Now I decided that it was now or never to ask. Stephanie might not leave me alone long enough to ask him afterward.

"Will you answer a question for me?" I asked as I served to Max. Once the birdie left me, I looked over to Cole, who just nodded his head slightly while he paid attention to the game.

"Why then?" He looked confused, so I explained. "If you just wanted it to be me and you, then why did you want Stephanie to come?" All the games instantly stopped when I finished asking, so Cole turned and started to walk to me.

"Because my friend is shy, and the only way he would go out with your friend is if I went with him. So it will be a double date, but only if Stephanie agrees to it." He got so close that all he had to do was whisper and I heard everything. I turned my gaze from Cole over to Max, and I saw the way he looked at Stephanie. Then everything clicked into place.

"It's Max." I turned back to Cole, who was still staring at me. "Am I right?"

With a sigh of relief, he said, "Yeah, you're right." We just kept on staring at each other until Coach told everyone to clean up and hit the showers.

I could feel the eyes of Max and Stephanie on us as they put their equipment away. I knew that it wouldn't be good for Max if he knew that we were talking about him. So I spoke louder so they could hear.

"I thought that you guys never learned how to spike the birdie yet?" He instantly knew that I was hiding our earlier conversation. But he joined in.

"I did my research, and my older brother was home for a couple of days. He showed me a few of his tricks." We didn't say anything else after that for several minutes.

"I'll take that for you." I forgot that I had the racquet in my hand until his hand was over mine. His hand was warm while he rubbed his thumb over my hand before taking my racquet and walked off. Stephanie was right beside me when he left.

"I don't think I should go on Saturday. I would be ruining it for both of you, apparently." As she said this, she looked like she was going to start jumping again. Probably thinking of what could happen in the future.

"No, you have to come." She gave me a questioning look. "Apparently, it's a double date, and before you say anything, let me finish." I took a deep breath before continuing as we walked to our spots in the change room. "Apparently, a guy in class likes you, but he's too nervous to ask you out, so he wants Cole there."

"Who is it?" Stephanie was quickly changed, so she waited for me to finish. I would have been quicker, but I couldn't wear my shorts after, and I really hated the cold.

"Well, I'm not sure if I should tell you who he is. I think he wants it to be a surprise for you. But I can tell you that he really likes you."

"Okay, I'll go. But if he's a dork or I just don't like him, I'm leaving right away." It then looked like she just remembered something really important. "Oh, hey, do you think you could give me a ride home today? My brother is taking the car so he can go shopping with his girlfriend again." She then looked like she was thinking of a plan, but before I could say anything, she was already telling me about it.

"How about I come over to your house, then we can pick something out for you to wear, then you can come over to my house and have supper there. My parents really want to meet you soon." I was finished getting changed during the explanation of her plan; we were walking to my car while talking. Coach let us out early for a job well done for today. We were six minutes earlier than normal.

"It's only Tuesday, Stephanie. Don't you think that we should wait until, I don't know, Thursday or Friday before we find an outfit for Saturday? It makes more sense. What happens if he cancels on Thursday? This way, if we wait, we won't have to deal with the disappointment." I started getting my keys out of my bag when I could see my car in sight.

"Yeah, okay. I guess you're right, but my parents still want you to come over tonight. My brother is gone for the night, so you don't have to worry about him." We were finally at my car, so I popped the trunk open for us to put our bags inside.

"Okay, I'll come over tonight. Just what time do you want me to come?" I unlocked my door and pushed the unlock button so Stephanie could get in. I looked over at Stephanie, and she had a huge grin on her face. "What?" She laughed, pointed behind me, and then she got into the car, leaving me standing there trying to figure what was up with her.

I was starting to get into my car when I heard Cole. "Hey . . . I'm glad . . . I caught you . . . before you left." He sounded breathless, and when he got to me, he put his hands on his knees to catch his breath.

"Hey, Cole. What's going on?" He took his right hand and pointed to the sky so I would give him a minute so he could catch his breath. *Wow, what was he doing to get so breathless so quickly?* Then I remembered that I've never actually told him that Stephanie said yes to the double date on Saturday. "I've talked to Stephanie, and she said yes for Saturday."

"That's . . . not why . . . I'm here."

CHAPTER 7

The Call

Cole was still leaning over his knees; his breath was getting back to normal quicker now. He straightened up and looked me in the eye.

"I wanted to ask you something else." He looked at my car and waved to Stephanie. While he was staring into my car, he kept on talking. "Although I'm not sure that I'm more or less excited about that. I did sort of want it to be just the two of us." He ran a hand through his hair, trying to get to the point.

"I wanted to ask you if you would mind if I came over to pick you up tomorrow." He leaned away from looking at Stephanie through the window and turned to me to see my current expression. "Of course, I'll understand if you want to drive yourself."

"No, I, um . . ." Then I wondered about Rebekah. "What about Rebekah?"

"What about her?" His face had gone all serious, and all signs of a smile had vanished right when I mentioned Rebekah.

"Well, doesn't she get a ride with you in the mornings? I don't think she'll be that thrilled about me getting a ride with you." Images of her throwing me out of his truck while it's moving sprang into my mind.

"I don't drive Rebekah here every day. Actually, I never do, except for yesterday. Her car broke down, and so she asked me to drive her, seeing as she didn't have a ride. And when she did,

I couldn't say no." Then he had a little hint of a smile on the edge of his mouth again. "Well, you know how nice I can be."

"Yeah, like helping a new girl gather her things together up off of the floor."

"Yup, like that." Then the hint of a smile left again as he said, "So I take it that you don't want to 'car pool' with me?"

"I never said that." A huge crooked grin spread across his face, and I knew what I was saying. "Oh, what the heck, Rebekah's already going to kill me."

"She's way too controlling for anyone in the world to handle. Don't worry though. I'll keep you alive." He then put his right hand over his heart and raised his left hand with two fingers straight. With a real serious face, he said, "I promise to you that I will do everything in my power to keep you safe from any type of danger." I couldn't help but laugh a little at him.

Then he relaxed and leaned forward to me until he was whispering in my ear. "I'll pick you up at seven tomorrow morning, and then we can go for breakfast—my treat." Before I could say anything back to him, he turned around and jogged over toward his truck that was surrounded by his friends. *Yup, Rebekah is going definitely going to kill me after tomorrow.*

With a deep breath, I looked through the group by his truck, looking for her; but I never saw her. *Maybe she already left, and she didn't see any part of what just happened.* I completely forgot about Stephanie until I heard a soft knock on the inside of my door.

I opened the door, and before I could sit down, she was asking me about what just happened. I didn't say anything until I started driving to her house, then I told her everything.

"Wow! You're here for only two days. And you get the hottest, most popular guy as your boyfriend." Stephanie finally leaned back and relaxed in her seat. She was hanging on to my every word as I told her what happened.

"He's not my boyfriend." I could feel the heat starting to rise to my cheeks. As I turned into her driveway, my mouth fell open. It was a three-story brick mansion.

"No, he's not." I turned away from the house toward her, and she had a guilty smile. "You're right. He's not—not until tomorrow morning, at least." Not wanting to talk about my maybe-relationship with Cole, I scanned my head trying to find another subject to talk about. Then I realized that I had an excellent subject right in front of me.

"So you actually live here?" We were parked in front of the glass double doors, so I turned off the engine. Stephanie nodded, and I continue with my subject change. "You must think that my house is . . . is . . ." I tried to think of a good way to phrase it.

"Cozy." I looked over and gave Stephanie a confused look. She just looked out of the window at the row of bushes. "Well, everything isn't spread all over the room. It's all close, so you don't have to do a lot to get something."

"Okay, I get your point about the space, but my house isn't cozy. I was thinking more of small, tiny, crowded."

"No! I like your house. In my opinion, it's the perfect size. You don't have to yell to get the other person's attention from another room. Believe me—it gets annoying and really boring living in a house like this." We were out of the car and making our way up the twenty stone stairs to the front doors.

"Well, then, maybe you should come over after school more and even have sleepovers during the weekends at my house." We were just at the door when Stephanie stopped dead in her tracks.

"Just to let you know, my parents aren't the best at minding their own business. Especially when someone they've never met before is around the house when they're home." She then took another step closer to the golden doorknob. She was hesitant about turning the knob to open the door into her own house.

"Hopefully, we can sneak by so they don't ambush you when just as I open the door." I looked up at the window above us, and I saw two backs as they retreated from there. I looked at Stephanie, who was taking a couple of deep, slow breaths. Her eyes were closed, and her hand hovered over the knob.

"Um, Stephanie." Stephanie looked toward me with a worried look, so I smiled, trying to get her to relax a little. "I don't think I can sneak by. I saw two people in that window." I pointed up at the window, and Stephanie looked up.

"I can't believe that they—" We were both looking up at the window when the front door opened wide, and her parents were standing just past the frame. "—are waiting for us to come in." Stephanie managed a small smile at each of her parents.

"Welcome to our home, please make yourself comfortable." Mrs. Ozone said with a warm, welcoming smile. She had a light pink short-sleeved floral dress that went to her knees. *Wow. I guess I will get to the temperature here. Hopefully soon though—I'm freezing my butt off!*

"Well, don't just stand there. Stephanie, why don't you show Britney around the house, so she knows where everything she needs is located." Mr. Ozone wasn't wearing a suit, but it looked a lot like he was. He was wearing all blue with a light gray shirt underneath his thin jacket. *Boy, do they always dress like it's the prom around here? No wonder Stephanie was warning me.*

"Thanks for having me over." It was all I could get out of me as I walked through the opened doorway into their front room. The room was pretty much empty except for several tables around the walls. Looking up, I saw a huge glass chandelier suspended in the middle of the room.

"It's no problem. We love meeting new people." While Mrs. Ozone was talking to me, Mr. Ozone came over to me and offered to take my jacket.

"Thanks." I gave him my jacket, and he put it over his arm just like in the movies. I wrapped my arms lightly over my chest, trying to keep the warmth from the jacket within me.

Looking over my shoulder, I saw Stephanie's face go red as she put her hands over her face as if she was embarrassed. *At least she has both parents around, and they care about her enough to spend time with her and her friends.*

"Supper will be ready in about an hour and a half, so you two can do whatever until then." Mrs. Ozone left us in the front room. She headed in the direction of another room. I could just barely see some pots on a stove.

"We can do our homework if you want, then you won't have to do it alone at your house." Stephanie grabbed my elbow and started to pull me up the snow-white stairs. I could tell that she was really embarrassed about her parents, so I went along willingly. When we got to her room, we sat on the floor and started our homework while talking.

"I say you'll get kissed by Cole no later than this weekend." We were halfway through our English before we even started talking about Cole.

"You don't know for sure. And we're not even dating." I closed my book and got out the notebooks for the next class.

"Then what do you call it? He even said it was a date to you, and you never corrected him." She forgot about school at the moment and watched me. I just kept my eyes on the notes. I could feel her eyes on me as I worked on copying them.

"That's because I don't want to be mean to him." I looked over to Stephanie, who had a giddy look on her face.

"Say what you want, but when you come to school tomorrow morning with him, it will be official." By the end, Stephanie started singing, and I felt my face get red. "You know what? I don't think anyone has gotten the most popular guy in school to ask her out in such a short period of time."

Just then the familiar saying "saved by the bell" screamed throughout my head as my cell silently vibrated in my front pocket. When I looked to see who it was, it said unknown caller.

"Who is it?" Stephanie had closed her books and was moving over to see who it was. She could also hear the conversation better.

"I don't know. I don't recognize the number, and there's no name." I studied the number before I realized that it was a number from town. Stephanie recognized the same thing about it. Only she didn't know who it was exactly either.

"It might be Cole." Stephanie was lying on her bed, looking over my shoulder at the number. She was trying really hard to think of who it could be.

"I didn't tell anyone my number." It was only on its fourth ring, so I knew that I had to answer it. I pressed the talk button and rested it against my ear.

"Hello?" I could hear someone's heavy breathing on the other end. But they didn't say anything. I waited for them to answer, but they never did.

"Who is this?" My voice was stronger now. I wanted to know who in this town got a hold of my cell number. That way I could tell whether or not I would have to change it again.

They still didn't answer. I could still hear the breathing on the other end getting harder and harder. My own breathing was getting harder just like theirs. Stephanie was still at my ear, and she heard the breathing too.

"Why aren't they answering you?" She moved over to my other ear to whisper it in so the person on the other line wouldn't hear her.

I tilted the phone away from me before I spoke. "I don't know." I kept my voice just as low as hers. I didn't want them to know that I was talking about them with them on the line. I pressed the phone back to my ear to try again. "Who is this?" *They aren't going to scare me.* In the background, I could hear a wolf howling.

The heavy breathing on the line was suddenly quiet for a moment. In the background, I could hear a train whistle blowing from a distance. The sound of metal hitting metal sounded through the phone. The whistle blew again. It was getting closer to the phone and the person on the other end. Any minute now, and the train would be past them.

The train whistle blew another long, loud blow. The wheels screeched as they tried to stop in time. The whistle kept on getting louder and lasting longer. *The person was committing suicide, and he called me before he did it.*

Stephanie was shaking my shoulder, trying to get my attention—it didn't work. I was too busy listening to hear if they were really doing what I thought to pay the smallest attention to what she was going to say.

The sound of the phone being crumpled by the wheels of the train was as loud as a helium balloon being popped right beside your ear.

I automatically pulled the phone away from me as the impact sounded in my ear through the phone. A minute after the screeching stopped, the phone on the other line wasn't producing any sound. The only sound was the dead sound of the line being cut off from the phone.

When the phone slipped out of my hand, Stephanie quickly grabbed it before it could hit the floor. I would have been grateful if I hadn't just heard someone die.

"Britney, what happened?" Stephanie got off of her bed and seated herself right in front of me. "Tell me what happened." Her voice was quiet and soft.

"They . . . they . . . died." My eyes were stuck on her white wall, so I didn't see her response to what I just said.

"How?" Her voice was quiet, and when I could eventually take my eyes off the wall, I saw her staring at the floor beside me.

"A running train. It was coming close, and they placed the phone on the rail. I think they went on it too. I don't know for sure." I pulled my legs closer to my chest and wrapped my arms around them. I tried to think of what just happened.

"Tell me everything. Exactly what happened?" She still didn't look at me, so I went back to staring at the wall.

"They stopped breathing as they set the phone down on the rail. I heard the train blowing its horn as it got closer. Then eventually, the wheels on the train were screeching to a stop as it got closer."

We were silent as we both took in what just happened. I just kept on running my hands over my legs.

"Girls, supper is ready whenever you are!" Both of us jumped when we heard Mrs. Ozone as she called us down.

I just barely heard Mrs. Ozone through the door. Stephanie and I quickly packed up our stuff and hurried downstairs to eat.

We didn't talk about the call all night.

CHAPTER 8

Car Trouble

"Thanks again for having me over. I had lots of fun." It was 8:00 p.m., and we were at the door saying good-bye. We finished eating over an hour ago, and Stephanie and I finished all of our homework after that. We both completely forgot about the call earlier that evening. At least, neither of us were willing to talk about it at the moment.

"No problem. I'll see you tomorrow at school, okay." Stephanie was the only one with me to see me off; her parents were still cleaning up. *How much do they have to clean?*

"Yeah, I'll see you tomorrow at school." Stephanie opened her mouth, and I knew what she was going to ask, so I answered her before she had to even make a sound. "And before you even ask, I'll tell you everything that happens tomorrow morning." Stephanie closed her mouth and nodded at me.

We were walking to my car while talking about it when I got a chill down my back. Not a cold chill from getting too cold, but a chill from being watched. I looked over at Stephanie to see if she noticed anything, but it didn't look like she did. "Do you have a feeling that we're being watched?"

"Yeah, I do. It's no big deal. My parents always watch through the windows when they can. They also pretend to be busy with something else, but they're really listening to every word you say. They know a lot of gossip about people in town, so they watch to see if it's true." I looked back at her house, trying to find her parents, but I didn't feel that I was being watched from there. It was more like someone was watching from the scenery around us.

"I'm not getting the feeling from your house." I looked around the property, but it was too dark to see if anyone was around to even see us. "I think someone else is here watching us." Stephanie was now looking around, trying to see if anyone is watching us.

"I don't see anyone." Stephanie reached in front of me and opened my car door. "And besides no one even knows where I live."

I grabbed the door from Stephanie when she was still talking. "What about Cole? He had to know in order to pick you up and when he dropped you off."

"Nope." Stephanie gave me a wide smile. "I was walking toward your house when he picked me up. I was about ten minutes of straight driving away from here. I also woke up around there as well and told him to drop me off there. I walked the rest of the way. So no one except my family and you know that I live here." I have to hand it to Stephanie. She can make sure no one figures out where she lives.

"How come you don't want anyone to know where you live? I mean—look!" I waved my free hand toward her house before continuing. "This is the nicest and biggest house around town."

"I know! I don't want anyone to know because they would only be my friend for my house and the things I have. I haven't even told the group about this." She looked down at the driveway and shuffled her feet slightly.

"Why not? I mean, you know that they'll be your friends even if you had a huge house. I mean, you haven't even known me for a whole week, and you've already shown me where you live."

"I don't know." She looked up, but she didn't look at me. She was staring at a bush not too far from us. "There's just something different about you." She looked up at the sky with a heavy sigh. "I don't know how to explain it. It's like I know that you won't judge me for what I have, but for who I really am." She then looked at me. "Anyways, you better get home. Your mom should be home by now, and I'm sure she's getting worried by now."

"I thought that you were sleeping when she got home." She gave me a sly smile while she answered.

"I was, until you got up. Then I was pretending." I gave her a dirty look, and she continued. "Also, I wanted to see what would happen if I was still asleep when Cole had to leave. Even though he obviously didn't want to leave you right then." She put her left hand on my shoulder. "I won't do it again, but maybe you should. You can feel his muscles through his jacket."

"Maybe the next time I have a chance." She looked pleased that I would try to get him to carry me. I went into my car, turned the key, and rolled down the window. "I'll see you at school tomorrow, and you should probably tell the guys where you live. They'll still be your friends."

"Yeah, probably, I'll think about it. Talk to you later." With a final wave to Stephanie, I rolled up my window and headed home.

•••

I was about halfway home when my car slowly stopped in the road. *Crap!* I looked over at the gas, but I still had half a tank left. "Why me! I'm not a mechanic." I reached in my bag, trying to find my cell to call CAA, but I came up empty-handed. "Don't tell me that I left my phone in Stephanie's room! Please!" Without my phone, I slammed my head on the steering wheel and tried to figure something out.

A few minutes later, I decided that I had to try to fix the problem by myself. *I should have taken that auto class last semester when I had the chance.*

I opened up the hood, trying to see the problem, but my eyes weren't adjusted to the dark yet. There were no street lamps around that I could use. The headlights were only showing me shapes.

I was trying to feel if anything was broken when my right arm slid into some car oil. It was smooth, sticky, and it went all the way up to my elbow. "Great."

"I told you, Amanda. I told you that your car will break down, and you'll need me to fix it." It was a male voice, and I wondered who else got their car stuck on the road. "So now you're not talking to me? Amanda! I won't rub it in, okay? Now let me help you before you either make it worse or you hurt yourself again." All of a sudden, I saw a figure leaning against my car, and I realized that he was talking to me.

"I think you're confusing me with someone else." I saw his body tense when he realized that I wasn't who he thought I was.

He then relaxed a little before he talked. "Well, I can still help you out with your car problems. That is if you want help from someone else."

I considered telling him, "No, thanks." But I really didn't have any other option, and my arm was starting to get even colder from the oil. "Sure, but I don't know what's wrong! It was working smoothly for months." I stepped away from the engine to let him take a look.

"Well, for starters, you need to wipe the oil from your arm." He handed me a small cloth, and I started to wipe the oil from my arm. "Then we need to get some light, so we can actually see what the problem is." I handed him the cloth even though I still had some oil on my arm and headed to the trunk for a light.

"This is the only one I got in the trunk." He laughed a little when I said this. I stopped dead in my tracks. No one else was here except for the two of us. "What?"

"I'm sorry. It's just that you look and act a lot like this person I know. And I'm sorry that I called you by her name." He turned toward my engine, and I turned on the light for him.

He was wearing black jeans with a matching black T-shirt. The T-shirt wasn't loose, and I could easily see some little muscles covering his arms. His hair was short to the ears, straight, and hardly dirty blond. He was also about a head taller than me. He turned toward me, and I saw his tree-bark eyes and his little pale skin and the shadow of dark rings around his eyes.

"If you want, I can tell you what to do next time this happens, in case you're by yourself." He motioned for me to come closer to actually see what he was doing to my car.

"Sure." I took a couple of steps toward the engine. "Hopefully, though, I remember my cell so I can just call someone for help." I leaned in, and I saw oil all over the place from my arm. "I guess I sort of made a mess on everything."

"It's okay. It could be worse, and by the way, I'm Leo Darkwood." I ran through all the people in my classes that I knew the names of, but I've never heard his name before.

"Hi. I'm Britney White." I stuck my hand out to shake his, but then I saw some oil on my hand and quickly pulled it back.

"Did you say that your last name was White?" He averted his eyes away from the engine to look at me. I couldn't think straight of what he was asking, so I just nodded, and he continued. "Do you have any siblings?" I shook my head, and he looked confused. "Where did you live before you moved here?"

It took me a moment to think straight enough to verbally answer him. "I used to live in LA." He slowly nodded at me, and he whispered the word "interesting" to himself.

"I think I got it all figured out now." He quickly turned to me. "Go turn the ignition, and I can see if I'm right." I did as he said and went inside my car. All the heat had evaporated within the car. When I turned my key, my car hummed to life. *Thank you!* I hopped back out and walked over to where Leo was shutting the hood and wiping his hands on the cloth.

"Thank you." I looked at his hands as he passed me my lit flashlight. There was a weird design on the palm of his hand. I had to slit my eyes to look at it better before I realized it was a black crescent moon. *I wonder if I should say anything about his tattoo.* I was deep into argument whether or not to say anything about it when he started talking.

"So you lived in LA your entire life. One day, you wake up and suddenly decide to move all the way up here. Also, your last name is White." He leaned against the surrounding tree and looked up while he finished talking.

"Very interesting, I wonder if it's just coincidence that—" All of a sudden, I saw an object fall down and hit Leo hard on the head before he finished. "Oww!" He started to rub his head when I realized that someone else was here.

"Are you okay?" I took a step closer to him, and I saw what was thrown at him. A long black high-heeled shoe was thrown at his head. "Who else is here?" I tried to look up the tree and see who it was. They threw a sheet of paper at Leo, and then they just jumped over the brick wall before I could see them.

"It's no one special, just an annoying friend." I looked back at him and saw that he was reading a note while he answered. "I better go though, I can't be late." He headed toward the wall, and I saw that he was heading for that weird building.

"What is that building?" I hadn't realized that I said this out loud until he stopped dead in his tracks and turned toward me.

"It's a school. Why do you want to know?" He took a couple of steps back toward me while he talked. "There's only one way to get in though. Hardly anyone knows about it. That's why no one in this town knows what the building is for sure. Well, except for the people that go here."

"So how do you get in?" He stopped walking toward me and held out his right hand.

"You have to have either a crescent moon, like me, or a full moon. You can only have one, and it's always on your right palm." He took another step toward me but more slowly as if he thought I would be scared of what he was telling me.

"So the only way you get into this school is if you have a tattoo of a moon on your hand. That must be some school." I crossed my arms over my chest to help keep warm.

"It is." He didn't look like he enjoyed being at the school. I looked at his face, but all I could look at was his eyes. They had a white layer over them, and he looked like he was very deep in thought. *Well, at least I know that I'm not the only one who gets deep in thought.* " . . . tell anyone you know!"

"Hmm? Tell anyone about what?" He started talking while I was thinking to myself. I only heard the end of what he was saying.

"You can't tell anyone anything about what I've just told you about that building. No one outside the building knows what it's used for." He put his left hand on my right shoulder and looked me in the eyes. "You have to promise me that you won't tell anyone anything." His eyes were hard as he watched me. After a moment, I had to turn away, only to return to looking at him.

"I promise I won't tell a soul what you just told me." His eyes narrowed like he was trying to see if I was seriously telling him the truth.

"I'll be around watching you." He looked up at the wall for half a minute then back at me. "I better go now. I'll see you later." Before I could say anything else to him, he was already running toward the unlocked gate.

CHAPTER 9

First Date

I woke up that morning tired beyond belief. I kept on having the dream where I'm in the forest over and over again. It wouldn't stop! No matter what I did, it still ended the same way—with the grizzly bear attacking me when he's done killing the guy.

I laid in bed just thinking about it. *I wonder why he doesn't run or put up any fight. I wonder what it means.* This wasn't the first time that I've had the same dream over and over. My friends always told me that it meant something.

Tired of just thinking about the dream and my past, I decided to get ready. When I got up, a part of my shoulder was warm and tingly from where Leo put his hand on me last night.

I got ready in a trance, remembering what I'd learned last night and trying to figure out what the dream meant. Last night, after I got home, I wrote down everything that happened so I wouldn't forget. I also wrote down the dream several times, and it all read the same thing.

> *I'm barefoot in the wet forest. See a guy in the shadows. He offers a hand to me. I can't talk but I want to. I see a bear stalking us. I look back at the guy. He looks so upset! The bear attacks him. I can't move! When the bear is done it turns to me. I still can't move! The bear jumps to attack me.*
>
> *I wake up trying to catch my breath. I wake up sitting straight in my bed. My eyes are always wet.*

When I was finally ready, I looked out of my window. To my surprise, a red truck was sitting in my driveway. *Crap! I completely forgot that he was coming today.* As I looked at the clock, I relaxed as I saw that he was early.

I opened the front door to see Cole standing in the doorway with his hand up and ready to knock. When I looked at him, he was looking at me with a huge smile growing across his face.

"Hey, I was just going to make sure that you were still coming." He lowered his hand to mine and took my bag from my hold.

"I'm coming. I just didn't set my alarm earlier. I couldn't sleep, so I just started to get ready." We were almost at his truck. I just kept on looking forward just in case he could see how tired I was.

"I'm sorry that you didn't sleep well." He lightly tossed my bag in the truck bed. He opened my door for me while he talked. "I've read something that said that a good, fresh, warm breakfast can keep you awake and perky for hours." He shut my door and ran in front of the truck to get in his side.

"You know, I think I've read that somewhere too. I think it was on a commercial for that breakfast energy drink." I just looked out of the window shield. Cole turned his key, and the truck roared to life.

"Right, it's the one with the bottle that danced everywhere when it came to life." Cole pulled out of my driveway, and we were off.

"I think you're confusing the commercial. The people start dancing, not the bottle. It's just an ordinary energy drink bottle."

"Really, because I'm—" When we drove past the Twiddle building that was apparently a really exclusive school, I couldn't help but look around for Leo. All I saw was the same tree; although nothing was there, I still couldn't help but stare at it, hoping to see him. "Britney?"

"Yeah?" *I must have blocked Cole out while I was looking for Leo.* I looked over at him; he had a concerned look on his face. He kept on watching me while he slowed the truck down so he could watch me longer without hitting anything.

"Are you all right, Brit? You look really tired, do you just want to go back home?" He wasn't looking at me anymore, but I could tell from his voice that he was worried about me.

"No, I'm fine. I just really need some breakfast. Then I should be back to normal." *Normal for a little while, at least.*

"That's good." He looked away from the road for a brief moment and at me while he continued, "They have the best food anywhere around here. You also won't be hungry for hours—it's very filling."

"Good. So what is it called?"

"It doesn't have a name." After I heard this, I couldn't tell if he was serious or if he just wasn't going to tell me. He had a smile on his face as he watched the road.

"It has to have a name." I kept on watching him. He just shook his head.

"I know the owners, Brit. They couldn't decide on a name. If you still don't believe me, then look." He pointed straight ahead of us. "Do you see a name on the red building straight ahead of us?" I looked ahead and saw a small red-bricked building that looked like it was closed. I really did look for a name, but like Cole said, there wasn't one.

"Okay, then what do you call it if it doesn't have a name?" I directed my attention back to Cole. I wasn't about to block him out again.

"Well, not that many people around town know about it. They like going to the ones that have been around for years. They also like the ones that are closer to their house, not the ones that are at the edge of town." He pulled up in a parking lot across the street from the building. "It's good that way, I guess." He took his keys out of the ignition and turned toward me. "Think of it this way—no one we know can come in and bug us while we're here."

"Right. That's pretty smart, you know." He smiled at me while he got out of his side. I followed his lead and got out of the truck.

"Well, I saw the way she looked at you in gym. So I thought that we should go somewhere she wouldn't know about." *I wonder if she smiled at me after she saw that Cole was watching her.* He took my right hand in his as we walked toward the dark brown wooden doors. "I've never taken anyone here, not even the guys, so we should be good."

When we walked through the doors, I was drenched in the smell of bacon, sausages, pancakes, eggs, and more. The room was dark near the windows, but you could easily see everything inside. There were a few tables around the room, with a huge table in the center of the room with food on it.

We walked over to a table by the far window, and I put my jacket on the chair. *I must look so weird with a jacket on around here.* The table had a bright red tablecloth with plates, glasses, and cutlery on, all ready to be used.

Cole grabbed the two plates in one hand, took my hand in the other, and led me to the center table before he let go. "The food here is the best. It's a shame that not that many people know about it. I keep on telling the owners that they would make a fortune just from the food." I didn't know how much food I could take, so I started taking a little of everything, but I was still starving for more.

"How much are we allowed to take?" As I said this, my stomach growled. Cole smiled at me, and my face went bright scarlet. *He obviously heard it.* As I looked back at the table, I heard Cole chuckle a little laugh that he tried to cover as a cough. I continued to look away from him. After he was done *laughing* at my stomach growling, I felt his hand on my elbow, and I could feel his warm breath move strands of my hair away from my ear.

"Don't worry, Brit. You can have as much as you want. It's all for us. I called and told them. There's going to be about five more people that are coming, for sure. They need to get rid of the food before it goes bad."

"That's good, because I'm starving." As if to back me up on my statement, my stomach growled again, and my face automatically went even redder.

"Relax." He rubbed his hand against my arm as he whispered in my ear. All of a sudden, I heard the door close; and as I jumped, Cole laughed a little while he continued to get his food.

When I saw who it was, I relaxed even more. *At least it's no one I know.* There were two girls standing in the doorway who looked exactly alike except for their height and hair. The one had her long wavy black hair let loose, so it went past her shoulders. She was a little shorter than the other one. The taller one had her streaked blonde hair up in a fancy updo that I could never do.

The two men behind them were also the same, except that one had their hair past their ears, and they weren't wearing the same clothes. The one wore loose brown pants and a black jacket, but his blue shirt wasn't loose at all. The other one wore a loose green shirt, jeans that looked like they were made just for him, and no jacket.

Both of the guys looked straight at me as I walked with my food in hand to my seat. The two girls also looked at me too, but they weren't staring at me like the guys.

"Do you know them?" I looked away from them, and I saw that Cole was sitting down and staring up at me. I went to my seat and sat while I answered him.

"No, I don't kn—" The door closed again, and I quickly looked over to see who it was. My mouth fell open. I saw Leo walk by us to the table where the other four sat. Closing my mouth, I pulled my attention back to Cole. "But I do know him." Cole looked him over and quickly looked back.

"How do you know him? I've lived here my entire life, and I've never seen any of them before." While he was talking, my stomach growled again, so I picked up some bacon and ate.

"I was driving my car last night, and it broke down on the road." I took a drink of my water and continued, "He passed by, and he stopped to help me out. I guess a lot of people are nice here." I remembered my promise to Leo and didn't want to get into any more detail about that incident. To show that I was done, I continued my comment from before. "I know him, but I've never seen the others." We continued eating for a while, continuing little conversations with each other.

While I was getting seconds, I heard someone from the other table come up to me. I ignored whoever it was and continued getting my food. I reached for the last bagel, but before I touched it, that person following me around the table took it.

"Hey." I turned around, planning to tell them that I wanted it. I saw Leo looking at the bagel in his hands. My face went red when I saw that it was him. *I so need guy help.*

"I didn't know that you knew about this place or that you had a boyfriend already." He never looked away from the bagel as he spoke.

"Well, I didn't, but I wasn't driving." Then I whispered, "And I don't have a boyfriend. Unless you talk to Stephanie, she'll tell you different." Leo looked up from the bagel and stared at me through his lashes, giving me a confused look.

"So you two aren't together that way?" My face went redder, so I just nodded. "Then this is just like a welcome meal?" Again, I nodded, and he gave a quick little nod while he went back to looking at the bagel.

"I better go so we aren't late for class." I turned around and Cole was heading over with my jacket. "I'll see you around, maybe." He looked at me and handed the bagel over to me.

"Don't you want your bagel? I only took it so we could talk. Personally, I don't see how people can eat them." I shook my head slightly, and he looked back at his friends. I followed his gaze and saw that they all were watching us while eating their food.

"It's okay, you can have it. And they are really good for you, so try one. And you can take one everywhere with you." I looked back at Leo, waved good-bye, and joined Cole in his truck.

CHAPTER 10

Notes

We got to the school with just minutes to spare. We were talking and laughing so much on the way back that neither of us paid any attention to the current time.

"So what are you doing tonight?" Cole was asking as we ran to my first class.

"Hopefully, I can finish copying my notes for my classes so I can give them back to everyone soon." We were almost at my class, so we slowed down, and I could hear Cole's heavy breathing along with mine. "I'll see you later, Cole. Apparently, you can't be late again, and I don't want to help you miss it." I looked over at Cole, but he was looking straight ahead.

We were silent the rest of the way to my class. The only sounds were our heavy breathing getting slower and the sound of our shoes hitting the smooth floor. We weren't the only ones in the hall though. There were also several students standing around talking to one another, not bothering to go to class at all.

When we got to my class, I couldn't hear Cole's breathing anymore, and my own breathing was slower and more silent. I headed into the open doorway, seeing Stephanie up at the chalkboard with her back toward me. I took one step away from Cole, but his hand caught my arm. I turned around, and he let go his hold of me.

"I'll see you later today." He held my gaze for a moment, but the warning bell rang. He wasn't making any motion to move and head to his own class.

"Okay, but you better go before you're late." I then turned him around and started pushing him off to the general direction of his class so he wouldn't be late. He started to laugh at my attempt to get him there on time.

I walked into the classroom while everyone was still talking. No one really noticed me coming in, except for Stephanie. She was still talking to Mr. Colin, but she was watching me the moment I walked in. Within a minute, she started to jump up and down in place with excitement. I ignored her and went straight to our table. It wasn't long before Stephanie was staring at me while she jumped like a bouncy ball in her chair.

"Tell me *everything* that happened. I don't care if I don't need to know because I want *everything*!" I laughed at her enthusiasm and decided to tell her about it. During that entire period, Stephanie and I talked about my breakfast with Cole. I also figured out that the school library was the best library in town, so I went there during lunch to do some research.

The library was a little bigger than the normal classroom. It had a light-gray carpet that was covered in dirt from people's shoes. On the far side of the room, I saw only three computers lined up together facing the wall. There were only about seven floor-to-ceiling stacks of actual books around the middle of the room. *And this is the best library around?* As a disappointed sigh left my lips and echoed in the room, I made my way to the only computer that was turned on.

I sat down in the wooden chair and entered my ID number and name. While I waited for the page to load, I grabbed some of my lunch and started to eat. It was ten minutes later when I finally had Google up on the screen.

I started off with something that should be easy. I typed in the name of the town and got over three hundred hits. *Wow, Silver Stakes is smaller than I expected. LA had millions of hits last time I checked.*

Within the first fifteen minutes of searching, I let out a tiresome sigh as I read more pointless information about the construction of some popular buildings. I went to the advance search and typed in Twiddle for the main building that I needed to know about. When I hit "enter," it turned out two hits on the building.

"What are you doing?" I jumped a foot off the chair and let out a little squeal. The voice came from right by my left ear. I spun around and saw Cole's face inches away from mine. "Stephanie told me that you were in here, seeing as I was going to eat lunch with you and you weren't there."

"Sorry." He was still close, so I just whispered.

"It's okay, there's always tomorrow." He leaned away as he talked and pulled up a chair beside me. "So what are you looking up?" He looked over at the screen and saw a picture of the Twiddle building, front and center. "Curious?"

"Yeah, mostly because it would of made a way better school than this one." As I leaned back in my chair, I saw him nodding his head. He was agreeing with what I was saying and what I was used to.

"It was going to be, but it didn't meet the right standards for a school." He looked away from the picture and back toward me. "There's not that much about it on the computer." He reached over and turned my computer screen off. "So I can tell you anything you want to know about the building, if you want."

"Really? Anything I want to know about the building?" It seemed too good to be true. Here was someone who doesn't have to, but does offer to give me information of the building.

"Really. Any question you have about anything." He looked away from me but looked quickly back with a small smile on his face. "But not right now." He grabbed my bag and started to get up.

"Why can't we do it now? It's the perfect time to talk about it." I stood up right in front of him and took my bag back.

"It's the perfect time to get to class before we're both late." I looked over my shoulder at the clock and saw that we only had four minutes to get to class. Cole took my hand and started leading me out of the library. "We can always talk during gym."

During math I could only think of questions I wanted to ask Cole. I couldn't wait until gym. I ripped a piece of paper out of my notebook and started to write my questions down so I could remember them.

What is the building?

I was going to write more, but it really depended on what the answer was. I shoved the paper over to him so he could answer.

It took him a while before he could carefully slide the paper back to me. I took the sheet and carefully opened it so Mr. Divident wouldn't hear.

It was supposed to be the school, but it never opened officially. It just sits there now. I guess it's a reminder of what they wanted the school to be.

Why did it close if it was supposed to be used? It makes no sense.

Apparently it didn't meet the school standards. The town spent over half of the money they were given just to build it. They ended up with nothing left to do anything major with it. They tried to sell it, but no one had that much money.

Does anybody still go into the building and use it?

There are some rumours going around. People say that they see people coming in and out of there every so often. I wouldn't believe them. I've never seen anyone, and people say things just to get attention. Some parents might be spreading some of them just to make sure their kids won't go in there to mess it up.

How did the rumours even start?

After the building was abandoned, people started to dare others to go into it, and once they went in, they weren't seen for hours. When they got asked what happened, they don't know what the other person is even talking about.

What would happen if someone saw you go in there?

Mr. Divident stopped talking when I passed the note back to Cole. I looked at him, wondering if we were caught. He had his back to us, writing out a long equation on the board. There was no way that he could have seen or heard me pass the note over to Cole.

"I want every table to work together and figure out this equation. You have fifteen minutes. I'll walk around to help answer anyone's questions." Mr. Divident turned around and looked over at everyone.

"Then in the last minutes in class, I will randomly select someone from each table to come to the board to write their version of the answer on the board." We started to copy down the equation in silence, and then the conversations started to erupt around the room.

"I don't know. I haven't heard anything about trespassers other than if they get caught, they have some sort of punishment." It took me a while to figure out that Cole was answering my question. "Will you answer a question for me?"

I kept on looking at the notes, trying to figure out how to do the equation on the board. "The best I can." Flipping my notes back and forth, I paid attention to what he was going to ask me.

"Well . . . do you understand the math at all without using the notes?"

"Maybe." I flipped from page to page, trying to figure out what to do first, but I couldn't figure it out. "Or . . . maybe not." I closed my notes and groaned. "I hate math."

"Here, let me help you." Cole took my pencil and paper and started to write more of the equation. I tried to follow what he was doing. My mind was confused after he wrote the first line.

"You're going to have to explain this to me." I looked up at him, but he just kept on writing.

"If he calls you to go up, you're going to need the answer." Cole looked up at me, and he must have seen the worry on my face because he started to rub my back. "Don't worry. I'll put notes on the sides—that way, you can answer any of his questions."

"So what was your real question?" Cole's hand froze over the page. He obviously thought that I wouldn't have caught how he stopped for a moment. That always gives the person away.

"What do you mean?" He avoided looking at me as he looked around the room at everyone else. As if looking for the right person to help him.

"If you were really were going to ask me about my math ability, you wouldn't have hesitated." He slowly raised his head to finally look at me.

"Brit, I—" Just then Mr. Divident walked in front of our table. We both turned to look at him.

"Ms. White, why don't you go up with the others and write your answer on the board." He motioned me up to the board with the others. My breathing started to rise slightly. *I hate this class!*

"Don't worry, Brit, you'll do well." Cole handed me the sheet of paper.

"You're just saying that. This way you don't have to tell me what you wanted to ask me—yet." With a groan, I started to make my way to the front.

"Completely right, Brit." His voice was just audible to me. When I looked back, I saw him leaning forward on his arms and smiling at me.

Thankfully though, Mr. Divident was just making up the whole question time thing. All of the ones who wrote it didn't have to answer anything. Everyone did only if they knew the answer. When I went back to my seat, the bell rang, and I said thanks to Cole for the answer.

"Do you think I should tell them tomorrow?" Gym was over again, so Stephanie and I were walking to my car. We agreed in gym that I would drive her home so she didn't have to rush to catch her brother before he left. This also meant that we could talk to each other longer.

"The sooner, the better, then it will all be done and over with." We were almost at my car, so I dug into my bag looking for my keys.

"I don't get why you just don't put them in your pocket." I pulled out my keys and saw Stephanie's mouth fall open. She finally got a look at my keys. "How many keys do you have?"

"I have a copy of all the ones my mom has. That way, I can do stuff if she's at work. I still have to take off the ones that I can't use since we moved. I think I'll put them on another one—that way, I still have them just in case I need them." We tossed our bags in the trunk and went to our sides.

"Why would you still need them? You're not planning on leaving soon, are you?" Stephanie just looked at me.

"No, I was trying to get my mom to reconsider for a while." This wasn't making things any better. "My dad still lives there. I think of it like this: I want to go back and visit my friends again soon. I'm not going to spend even more money on renting a place or anything." I started to fiddle with the keys.

"Most of my stuff is still in my old house. I really want to get it all in one place. I can't convince my mom to move back, so I'll have to go down at some point to get it all." Stephanie understood and left it at that. I think she could tell that I didn't really like talking about it.

After I unlocked the doors, I noticed a piece of paper flapping in the wind. It was wedged in my window. I don't know how it got so far in. I looked around the parking lot to see if anyone was around. No one was, so I looked to see if any other vehicle that was left had one on there's. No luck.

"Britney, what's wrong?" Stephanie walked over and saw the note on my window. She didn't make any move to take it from the window. I didn't even really want to take it.

Realizing that we were both just staring, I took the note carefully off my window. Stephanie was still by my side. She looked eager to see what was written on the note. When I opened the note, I was shocked at what I saw.

CHAPTER 11

Cookies

Saturday

It was the only word on the page, but I still had to read it several times before I actually read it.

"Britney, what does it say?" Stephanie's voice was coming right in front of me, and as I looked up, she was staring at the note.

"Sa . . . Sa . . . Sa . . ." I took a deep breath and tried again. "It says Sa . . . Sa . . ." I wasn't going to try again. For some reason, I couldn't say the word. I just handed her the paper.

"Britney, it only says Saturday." I nodded, not expecting my voice to work properly at the moment. "It looks like someone's reminding us. Hey, I wonder if it was your date or mine that . . ." Her smile faded when she looked up from the note.

"Britney, are you okay? Your face is as white as the first snowfall in winter." She took a step closer and lightly pressed her hand to my forehead. She shook her head when she didn't feel any difference in my temperature.

"I'm fine. You might want to wait until I've actually seen snow firsthand before you start to compare me to it." I took a step away, and her hand fell to her side. "Like you said though, it was probably one of the guys just reminding us." I took the note from her hand and shoved it into my back pocket.

She just shrugged her shoulders and headed back to her door. As she walked away, I got a cold-to-the-bone shiver down my spine. I looked around the parking lot again, but no one was there. Trying to shrug and forget about it, I got into the car carefully.

"You're probably right. But wouldn't they just tell us instead of writing a note and putting it on my window?" I turned my key, and my car came to life. Once my music started, I reached over to turn it down so we could hear each other better.

"Maybe they would, if it was Cole. Maybe it was my date trying to remind us? Seeing as no one is telling me who he is." She looked straight ahead and thought for a moment. Just when I hit the road, she turned her attention back to me. "It is a guy, right? I don't want to go if it's a girl asking me out. That's just weird to me."

I started to laugh, which didn't help Stephanie relax from the question. It also didn't help the sick feeling I had in my stomach since I saw the note. "Relax, it's definitely a guy. I wouldn't think you were the type to go with a girl."

"But you do know who it is?" I kept my eyes on the road, but I could feel her baby blues on me, pleading with me to tell her more about her date.

"I know who it is, but I can't tell you." I looked from the road toward her. She looked down at her folded-up hands. "I promised Cole that I wouldn't tell you, and I always keep my promises the best that I can."

She looked up, and I gave her a very comforting smile. "But I can tell you that you know him from class."

"That doesn't help. I have a class with almost every guy our age." She folded her arms and rested her head against the seat. Her eyes still stayed on me.

"That's why I can tell you that, but nothing else." The rest of the ride to my house consisted of Stephanie asking me questions about her date. I did my best to be honest with her without breaking my promise with Cole.

When we got into view of my house, I stepped on the brake. I didn't know what I was seeing for sure, but something moved on the wall. I looked even harder and saw that it was a person scaling down the building. They were also leaving my open bedroom window. *My window hasn't been open since I got here.* I pulled the car quickly to the side and hopped out as quickly as I could before Stephanie's voice reached me.

"What are you doing?" I looked back and saw that she was stretching across the seat to see what I was doing.

"Just stay here, I have to check something out first. I'll meet you inside." I tossed the keys on my warm seat. "Can you put my car in the driveway for me? The house key is the one in light blue. Just let yourself in if I'm not there to unlock it from the inside." Without seeing what her reaction was to that, I headed over to my bedroom side of the house.

I looked around looking for the person that I saw leaving my room, when a warm hand landed on my shoulder. With a jump and a squeal, I turned around and stepped away from the hand. "Do you get your laughs by scaring me half to death every time you see me?"

"Sorry, but you know, it's kind of fun. Same reactions, same sayings, it's definitely true." I automatically relaxed as I realized that Leo was the one that put his hand on me. But then he said the last sentence, and I was confused.

"What's definitely true?" He looked away from me and shrugged his shoulders.

"Nothing, I talk gibberish sometimes." He kept on looking past me. It felt like he wasn't even talking to me.

"I'll remember that." I walked by him and remembered that I saw someone leaving my room. I quickly turned around and saw that Leo was staring up in the tree with his back toward me. I thought that I would scare him half to death before I asked him what he was doing here.

I walked quietly as I could as I got closer and closer to Leo's back. I was about to put my hand on his shoulder when he turned around.

"How come you aren't with your friend?" With my hand falling to my side, I took a deep breath. *Maybe I'll get him next time.*

"Were you in my house?" I wasn't going to answer his question before I got to accuse him for being in my yard.

"No, why would I go into your house without you there? It makes no sense." This time, when he talked, he kept on watching me. Then I remembered that he was talking to a friend that I've never seen yet.

"Then who came out of my room?" When I asked him this, his face went from friendly to very serious in an instant. I also got a sick feeling in my stomach again as his face changed.

"Someone was in your room? When?" Ignoring the sick feeling in my stomach, I actually believed deep within that Leo wasn't in my room. He just happened to stop by probably to see if my car stopped anytime after he fixed it.

"I'm pretty sure they were in my room, seeing as they left through my window. My window is never open up here. I saw them leaving when I was almost in the driveway." Leo looked away from me and toward my window.

"Mind if I come in then?" He looked back at me, and his face was softer than before but not entirely back to the friendly stage. "That way I can maybe tell you who he was. That, and someone might still be in there." Warning sirens went off in my head when he said that.

I just sent my best friend in there. Without even answering him, I turned around and ran to the front door as fast as I could. Barging in, I quickly looked around, but Stephanie was out of sight.

"Stephanie? Where are you?" Checking the first place I could think of, I ran into the kitchen, hoping to find her in one piece.

When I stepped in view of the kitchen, I saw Stephanie reading another one of my mom's note. "There you are." She looked up, and I saw that she was on the brink of crying. "What's wrong?"

Taking a step closer to her and the note, my stomach started to turn in an unpleasant way. When I got closer, she quickly took the note and shoved it in her back pant pocket without letting me see it.

"I don't think that you want to read it." Stephanie wiped her hand across her eyes, and I saw that she was already crying before I even saw her. "I also grabbed your newspaper from the steps." She grabbed the folded up paper and handed it to me. She was trying to distract me from the unread note.

I unfolded it and went to the table by the door. My mom always reads it when she got in. I didn't make it past the ark from the kitchen.

On the front page was a news report about a death that turned up only a few houses away from here. A picture was shown in black-and-white, but you could see every detail that it was showing. You could even see the details that you weren't supposed to see.

The man's eyes were closed, but his mouth was wide open. Liquid was flowing out of his mouth at the time of the picture. He had glasses that had snapped on the bridge, but was still on his nose. His hair was askew on the one side along with his clothes. That wasn't what got my attention in the first place.

On the side of his neck were two puncture wounds. Blood could have been the only thing coming out of them. The holes were smaller than a penny, but there was no indication of how deep they went into his throat. There was some of his blood that was smeared around the wound.

I quickly turned around and saw her watching me. "Who is this?" I read the name just as she said, "Devon Wood." "Did he have a BBQ at home?" I kept on reading as she talked.

"No, his family is vegetarians. They only use natural things. They had a campfire in their backyard though." She came up behind me and took a look at the article.

"That's funny—they state that he was murdered in the throat by a BBQ fork. They never found one though, but they did find some saliva around the wounds." I raised my head to watch her reaction to what I was saying.

"I don't get it. Whose saliva is it?" The tears were ceasing as she thought about this. We both forgot the note. I scanned the article, looking for the right name.

"Some guy named Tim Morency—do you know him?" Once I said his name, Stephanie's eyes bulged, and her mouth dropped.

After she closed her mouth, her eyes stayed bulged as she got a glimpse of someone behind me. She slowly raised her hand and pointed behind me.

Leo was standing behind me with a dark blue box in his hands. "I found this, and I can tell that it's not supposed to be upstairs in your room because of what's inside it." He looked up at Stephanie and nodded. She waved and started to shove me out to the living room.

"Are you nuts? Who is he? Why was he in your room? What about Cole?" There were no more signs that she was going to start crying again.

"What about him? Leo is just a friend, and will you please let me see the note?" I held out my hand for her to give me the note.

Exhaling a defeated sigh, she reached into her pocket and took out the note. "How do you even know him?"

"Does it really matter? I mean, I can meet new people outside of school." She handed me the note, and I opened it to read:

Britney,

Sorry that I had to leave so soon. I had no choice at all. It was this or I lose everything. You understand, right? My work requires me to be away from home for a while. You won't be able to reach me, and I won't keep in contact. I've already left, so you can't try to change my mind.

Love you☺

I could feel fresh tears starting to form in my eyes. I looked up, and Stephanie was by my side with a look of sympathy on her face. She had her arm across my shoulders and was rubbing my arm with her hand.

"I'm so sorry, Britney." Tears started to fall from her eyes again, and I did the exact same thing for her. After a moment of standing there like that, Leo walked into the room with the box.

"Is there anything I can do to help?" He walked over to us and pulled both of us into an embrace. He smelled like a fresh tropical breeze went though him. I didn't want to leave.

"I can't believe that your mom would just leave like that?" Leo let go of us, and I sat down beside Stephanie on the couch.

"I know. I mean, she's not around that much since I turned thirteen, but she still left me notes to communicate." I took another look at the note, and something popped out at me. "This letter isn't in her writing."

"What do you mean?" I stood up and went to the kitchen to grab another one of her notes. We always keep all the notes. They make a good reference to any argument.

"I mean that she didn't write the note." I shoved the drawer closed, then I ran to the living room to prove my point. "Do you remember the writing on the note that you saw last time?"

"I think so, why?" I handed her both notes and turned to explain to both of them what I was thinking.

"My mom doesn't draw smiley faces at the end, even if it's really bad news. That, and she also handwrites them, not computerizes them." I plopped down on the couch with a confident smile on my face. "So it couldn't have been my mom."

"Then who wrote it?" Leo took a seat on the arm of the chair across from us.

"No clue. So what was in the box that you came down with?" Leo got up from the chair and got the box from the kitchen. When he came back, he set the box down on the table.

"Why don't you open it up and see for yourself?" He looked at his watch and gave a sigh of disappointment. "I better go before I'm late again." He looked down at us on the couch. "I'll see you later, Britney. And it's nice meeting you, Stephanie." He gave a little nod and left the house.

"I wonder where he goes." I didn't realize that I was staring after him until Stephanie started to wave her hand in my face.

"Remember your boyfriend, Cole?" I looked away from the door down to the box.

"He's not my boyfriend, and no matter how many times you say it, it doesn't change that fact." I got up from the couch and grabbed the box before I sat down again.

The box was smooth and warm in my touch. It was no bigger than a piece of paper, yet it was heavier than a basketball. Written on the box was a little note.

Hope you enjoy a treat that I made for you!

There was no doubt about it. My mom put this where ever Leo had found it. I slowly lifted the lid of the box with Stephanie by my side. When I opened the lid far enough to see inside, Stephanie let out a little squeal.

"Cookies! I can't believe that you got homemade cookies." I was intrigued by the smell of freshly made cookies that I couldn't move. A single tear tell from my eye. Stephanie noticed.

"What's wrong?" Stephanie returned to her position in comforting me, and I couldn't help but smile at her.

"My mom never does this type of thing. It just caught me by surprise, I guess." Another tear was about to come, so I quickly got up to go to the bathroom. "I'll be right back."

"Okay, take as much time as you need." Stephanie started eyeing the cookies, and I couldn't help but laugh at her. My laugh was shaky to my ear. I didn't know if Stephanie heard it though. It sounded like I was forcing the laugh, and the tears were taking over. She was still watching the cookies like a kid with presents under the tree.

"Just leave me some." She nodded in agreement, then I left for the bathroom.

Looking in the mirror, I saw that my face was almost exactly like when I woke up from the dreams, although my hair wasn't a mess like then. I liked that fact.

After a few minutes, I decided that I'd left Stephanie alone long enough. Before I went back out, I took a few deep soothing breaths. And to my luck, it also calmed my stomach down a little bit.

When I stepped down from the stairs, both Stephanie and the box were gone. I heard the sound of the fridge opening and closing several times, so I guessed she was in the kitchen going through the fridge for something. I was right. She had two glasses filled with milk and the box of cookies in the middle.

"You didn't have to do that." She looked up from placing the glasses down and smiled at me.

"Yes I did. I already had three, and they are really good with milk." Stephanie lifted her glass to me as I walked to the table.

"All freshly made cookies are good with milk." I took a seat in one of the chairs and grabbed a cookie. "I remember, when I was little, she would make a whole batch of just cookie dough and we would grab a spoon and start eating it like that. Then whatever we couldn't finish, we would bake." I looked up from the cookie that I was fiddling with and looked up at Stephanie. "This was before her job got in the way of us doing stuff together."

Stephanie stopped in the middle of the bite and just looked at me. Her face was a little paler than usual, and her eyes had a watery layer over them. After a moment, her hand started to shake.

"Stephanie, are you okay?" The only movement she made was her hand shaking. I stood up and quickly went to her. Her whole body was shaking and was covered in sweat. It wasn't long before Stephanie's head fell to the table.

CHAPTER 12

Waiting Room

"Oh my, Stephanie! Stephanie, can you hear me!" I shook her gently, but after several good shakes, I started to panic. *Hospital. I have to get her to the hospital.* Looking down at Stephanie, I realized that I wouldn't be able to carry her all the way to my car.

Running around the house looking for the cordless phone, I wondered if the cookies were really from my mom. *I can deal with that later! I need to call an ambulance!*

When I found the phone, I had a problem trying to dial. My hands were shaking so much that I couldn't press the right numbers. After the fourth time, I got it.

"Nine-one-one, what's your emergency?" It was a girl that was talking to me. She sounded like she hasn't slept in several hours.

"I need an ambulance right away." I ran back to Stephanie and rested my hand on her forehead to check her temperature.

"What's the problem?" She sounded more awake than before, and I was relieved that she was taking me seriously.

"My friend is shaking, sweating all over, and silently gasping for air. I don't know what's wrong." I quickly got up and ran a cloth under some cold water to put on her head as I was talking.

"Okay, what's your location?" She was taking me completely serious now. It could be from my tears in my voice.

"Twenty-nine Stone Street, Silver Stakes." I wasn't sure if the cold water was working for sure, but I got a groan from Stephanie. I kept the water on her forehead.

"I'll send someone over right away. Don't move her." With that demand, the phone went dead in my ear.

I dropped the phone and put all of my attention on trying to bring her temperature down. I kept on talking to her for several minutes before I heard the sirens of the ambulance coming from a distance.

I quickly got up from the chair and ran to the door. It was them, all right. I waved them in and moved to the side, telling them everything that happened to her after she went pale.

They took her temperature and blood pressure right there. Then the one guy went back out to the ambulance. Within a minute, he was back inside pulling a stretcher behind him. The two guys lifted Stephanie up on the stretcher and told me that I should come to, just in case she woke up on the way to the hospital.

In the ambulance, the guy worked on Stephanie while asking some questions to me. I could tell that I wasn't looking so good either when he handed me a water bottle. I took little sips in between, telling him the information that he needed.

When we were halfway there, the driver told me that I should call her parents to let them know what was happening right now. I was so relieved that I programmed her home number into my phone. This time, I called them a lot quicker.

"Hello, Ozone residence." I could tell from the simple sound of the voice exactly who I was talking to at the moment.

"Mrs. Ozone, it's me, Britney."

"I'm sorry, Britney, but Stephanie isn't home right now. I'll let her know that you called." She was about to hang up, so I rammed everything together.

"She's with me, and we're on our way to the hospital." Everything went silent on the other side of the line. We were getting closer to the hospital, and I didn't want to leave Stephanie alone yet.

"Mrs. Ozone?" I waited for a moment, but there was no answer. "You might want to come down to the hospital. We're pretty much there, and I don't want to leave her alone. Just in case she wakes up. I'll explain everything better when you get here." With that, I was told to hang up, so I didn't interfere with any of the equipment inside. I followed their instructions exactly.

I ended up sitting in the waiting room when Mr. and Mrs. Ozone came in. They weren't wearing any coats, so I imagined that they were in too much of a hurry and forgot them. I stood up from the chair and started making my way toward them.

When they saw me, they both came rushing over. Mr. Ozone got to me first and held me at arm's length as he watched fresh tears falling from my eyes.

"What happened?" His voice was cracked.

"It just happened so fast." They looked at each other, and I could tell that they thought the worst. I felt horrible for even giving the slightest idea. "She's okay. They say that it wasn't as bad as they thought." They both relaxed a little. Mr. Ozone let go of my arms to walk over to the front desk to ask the nurse standing there some questions.

Mrs. Ozone led me to the couch, and we both sat down. She didn't say anything to me as we waited for the latest update on Stephanie.

"I'm sorry." It was all I could come up with to say to her. It was only a whisper, yet it seemed to fill the entire room. She put her arm around me as she talked.

"It's okay. Does your mother know that you're here?" She handed me a Kleenex, and I blew before I answered.

"No, she doesn't. I left so quickly that I didn't have a chance to leave a note if she got home." I looked over to her, but she was just staring at the door, waiting for Stephanie to walk through the double doors.

We weren't the only people in the waiting room. There were about two other families in there other than us. From what I heard, the two boys had a collision—both were drunk and severely hurt.

I looked up to the white-and-black clock that hung over the cream-colored double doors. It was 6:45 p.m. I've been seated for two and a half hours so far, and there was no new news about Stephanie.

It wasn't until 7:15 p.m. before a doctor came straight to the waiting room. Mr. Ozone was seated in the middle of us and comforting Mrs. Ozone when we saw him come over.

"Mr. and Mrs. Clarkson?" All three of us let out a silent breath of relief and frustration while the family heard the outcome of their son. I couldn't handle it. I needed a break from all this.

"I'm going to go and call my mom so she doesn't worry about me." I stood, and when I did, I felt the blood rush to my legs. Both of my legs were deep asleep. I just stood there for a moment, waiting for them to wake. "Get me if there's anything new with her, please."

They both nodded at me like I was an idiot for even asking. I gave an apologetic look to both of the other families as I passed both of them. Both families were here long before I was.

When I stepped outside the motion-sensing doors, a rush of arctic wind came over me. I shivered like crazy, but it felt nice on my skin. I took several deep breaths, and I could feel the cold air go through my lungs. It helped me relax a little.

I opened my cell phone and waited for it to turn on. It only took a moment. I dialled home and waited and waited. I was about to hang up and go back in when someone answered.

"Britney?" There was worry and concern in the voice. It wasn't my mom though.

"Who is this?" I wrapped my one arm over my chest to keep me warm as I talked.

"It's Cole. Where are you?" His voice was relaxed, but it still had some tension and worry in it.

"What are you doing at my house? Is my mom there?"

"She's here. She didn't know where you were. I was going to come over since my practice was cancelled at last minute. I thought that I would help you study for the math test on Friday. She answered the door and asked me if I knew where you were. Where are you?"

"Can I talk to her, please?" I could feel the tears forming in my eyes again as I listened to him.

"Sure, just give me a moment." As I waited, I heard the sound of the dishwasher being turned on. *She was doing the dishes?*

"Britney? Where are you? Are you okay? What happened?" She had the same amount of worry, concern, and tension in her voice as Cole did. Maybe even more worry than him.

"Relax, Mom. I'm perfectly fine. Just a little shaken up, that's all." I heard a sigh of relief leave her mouth, and I was glad that she was a little relaxed for the moment.

"Where are you? You left your car here. You didn't even leave a note for me like you usually do." She was a lot calmer than before.

"There was a little accident. I'm here at the hospital with Stephanie." I heard something fall and hit the ground with a thud. I tensed just in case it was her.

"I'm on my way, baby. Do you want to talk to Cole again?" I deeply wanted to talk to him, but I also wanted to get back in there.

"I would, but I want to get back in there, just in case there's something new about Stephanie." I knew that he would definitely come seeing. She wouldn't know where to go. Then I could talk to him.

"I understand, baby. I'll be there as soon as I can. Love you." Without me even saying anything back to her, she hung up.

I turned my phone off completely and just stood there with my arms wrapped around me. After a moment or two, I got too cold for my liking. When I headed back in, I was disappointed at what I saw and heard.

No one in the room moved a single muscle since I left. There also was absolutely nothing new about Stephanie's condition. *It's like I never left.*

I sat down in the same spot and tried to stay calm. It wasn't long before my mom and Cole walked in from the outside door. I stood automatically and walked over to them. My mom got to me first.

She hugged me in a too-tight-for-proper-breathing hug. I couldn't breathe well during it, but I didn't mind.

"Are they Stephanie's parents?" She whispered in my ear while we hugged. I didn't have that much breath in me, so I just nodded. She slowly let go of our embrace and walked over to them.

Cole was next in line.

He didn't say anything at first. He just took my arm and pulled me closer to him for a hug. His was a completely new experience than my mom's.

He held me gently in his arms. Like I was a glass sculpture and even the slightest amount of pressure would break me. I could breathe easily in his embrace.

I took a deep breath. The smell of pine trees overwhelmed me. He smelled amazing.

I closed my eyes while breathing in his smell, remembering the walks in the park back home. He rubbed my back gently with both of his hands. Even more tears started to fill my eyes.

It wasn't the fact that I just realized that we were a couple. I liked that idea. He was the first relationship that I ever had. It was just the fact that no one ever hugged me like that before.

Just then the doors opened again, and the same doctor from before stepped out. We automatically guessed that it was for the other family. I could still see the worry and hope on everyone's face. I didn't want to leave Cole's arms, so I just turned my head to get a better look. My head was resting on his chest, and I could hear his every heartbeat.

The doctor looked at everyone in the room with an exasperated look. He walked to the middle of the doorway and paused to look at everyone.

"Mr. and Mrs. Ozone?" My body tensed when he said their names. Cole started to rub my back again, trying to get me to relax. He let go and took my hand as we walked closer to the doctor to hear the current results of Stephanie.

"What's going on? How's Stephanie?" Mrs. Ozone was being held by Mr. Ozone. My mom was behind them, with a hand on both of their shoulders. When we stopped walking, Cole put his arm around me and started to rub my shoulder.

"Your daughter is having a positive reaction to the medication we have her on." He paused and looked up from the clipboard. "Does she have an allergic reaction to anything?"

"She's allergic to nuts." Mr. Ozone answered, and I saw tears fall down Mrs. Ozone's cheeks.

"We thought so." He scribbled something down on the clipboard. "We've found some in her bloodstream along with a high lead level." He looked down at his chart, and it felt like a needle was being punctured into my stomach over and over. *I did this to her.* It was all that was going through my head as he told more facts about Stephanie's current condition.

"In the meantime, I suggest that you all go home for now. We'll call if there's any major difference in her condition, but you all should get some sleep for now. She won't be waking up for a while." With a final look at the charts, he headed over to the last family that was there. We all just stood there frozen.

After several moments, my mom walked over to my side. She placed a hand on my cheek.

"Come on, baby, you need some rest. There's nothing anyone of us can do now but to wait." She looked over to Mr. and Mrs. Ozone while they started at the doors. "Can we give you a ride home?"

"No, thanks, we have our car here." Mr. Ozone answered us, but his gaze stayed on the doors. Mrs. Ozone didn't say anything to any of us until we told her that we were going.

When we got to the car, Cole opened the door for me and whispered, "Everything will be fine with Stephanie. From what I know about her, she's tough." I nodded to him and went in the seat. I dozed off in the middle of Cole telling my mom where to go. He was the official backseat driver.

I shifted after a while; I felt the freezing breeze on my skin. I opened my eyes to see Cole smiling down at me. *Well, I at least did what Stephanie told me to do, even though she wasn't here to see it for herself.*

"She must be so exhausted after everything that happened today." I heard my mom trying to unlock the door with her keys.

"It's the one in light blue, Mom." She looked over her shoulder at me and smiled a sweet smile that told me that she wanted me to get some sleep. I looked up to Cole and saw that he was still watching me. "You can put me down now, Cole."

He just kept on watching me like he was happy with carrying me to my room. I started to get down, but Stephanie was right about the muscles. I couldn't move. Too tired to keep on struggling, I stopped and rested my head against his chest, breathing in the scent of pine trees with every breath I took.

Then I started to dream.

CHAPTER 13

Teams

I wasn't in the forest again. I couldn't hear the rushing water or smell the surrounding flowers. I was relieved when I realized that. But it was freezing cold and pitch-black. I couldn't even see my hand in front of my face.

There was a smell of evergreen trees that surrounded me as I stood there. I could hear a faint *tick-tick* sound that came out in front of me. I didn't know what it was from.

I couldn't stop myself from walking forward to see what it was. A couple of steps forward, and the ticking sound grew louder. Out of nowhere, I stumbled over something on the ground.

All of a sudden, there was light all around me.

When I looked at what I tripped over, I was petrified.

A piercing scream escaped my lips when I saw that it was my body. I quickly backed away from it as fast as I could before my back hit a surrounding tree. I frantically looked around, trying to find a way out. I was surrounded by trees so tight together that a mouse couldn't even get through them. I slid down the tree until I was on the ground. I was trapped in the clearing.

The only other person in the circle was my dead body. Taking a deep breath, I looked at the body just to make sure that it was me, not my imagination.

My eyes and mouth were open, and all color had left my face and eyes. I was wearing a red T-shirt and a pair of low-cut jeans. My hair was fanned out thinly, like a piece of paper.

I slowly started to get up, but then I heard laughter. Looking around the trees, I never saw anyone coming. The laughter grew louder. I realized that it was coming from above.

When I glanced upward, I saw a guy fall from the sky. Not the actual sky, but he jumped from a tree branch into the opening. He landed right behind the body facing me.

Trying to get a hold on myself, the light dimmed around both him and me. He didn't even notice that I was there, watching.

He just stared at the body. I saw saliva slowly slide down from the side of his mouth as he leaned toward the body. A low growl stared to emerge from his chest the closer he got to it.

I watched as he bent over the face. He smelled the neck before he licked it just below the jaw. His eyes were closed, but when he opened them, he stared at me with his bright gold eyes. My breathing quickened as he stared at me.

He didn't say anything, but a sly smile slowly spread across his face. He leaned over the body and closer to me. I didn't move a muscle as he watched me from the other side of the body.

After a moment, he slowly started to get up. There was a little red line that went down his chin that wasn't there before. His eyes never left me as he walked over the lying body.

I reached behind me, hoping that there would be a break in the tree or something that I could use to stop him from getting closer to me. But there was nothing in feeling distance.

He was almost at me when he leaned forward and slowed down. It was like he wanted me to try to run. To try to make it more fun for him. When I didn't start to get up, he started to come closer and closer. He was steadily closing the long gap of ground that separated us.

He was a foot away from my feet when he stopped. He tilted his head slightly as he showed his sharp pointy teeth for me to see. There was some red on the ends of each tooth.

He crouched right down to the ground, ready to strike. I couldn't move. I looked past him and saw the head of the body move to look at me.

There were two small round holes on the side of her neck that had blood flowing down the side. She looked straight at me. "Choose wrong, and it will happen to you." Her voice was harsh, and tears fled from her eyes. All of a sudden, the body turned to dust and sank into the ground. The only other remains of her were a gold necklace, a silver bracelet, and several rings.

My attention went straight back to the guy. He started to laugh as he got into a fighting position like a lion before he sprang on his prey. There was complete silence all around us, and as he sprang forward, the sound of bells rang loud and strong.

Gasping for air, my eyes popped open. When I saw the brightness in my room, I sat straight up. *Am I late?* I looked over to my alarm clock and saw that it was going off for ten straight minutes.

I sprang from my bed and got ready for school faster than ever. When I ran by the kitchen, I froze. Thinking and remembering what happened to Stephanie last night, my stomach turned. Today was going to be completely different without her.

●●●

I was right. My first period was dead boring without her. Leah wasn't back, so I was the only one at the table. Everyone knew that something was wrong when she didn't show up, but they just thought that she was sick. *I thought that news travelled faster in a small town.*

When I walked into the cafeteria, everyone was engaged in conversations. I walked over to our table, and everyone there watched me. We all ate our lunches for several minutes before we ended up talking.

"We heard what happened." Melanie moved her chair closer to me but not exactly where Stephanie always sat.

"Who told you?" I just sat there, watching the guys talk while they ate.

"Cole mostly told us." I looked over to her, but she was looking down. "Stephanie doesn't tell us everything that we should know. I didn't even know that she was allergic to nuts either."

"She also got violent lead poisoning from the cookies too." When I said this, both of the guys dropped their conversation and stared at me. "Cole didn't mention that fact, did he?" They all shook their heads, then the guys gave an annoyed look over my head. I turned to look, but Cole pulled up a chair beside me and joined our group as I did.

"So what are we talking about?" Cole glanced around the table at everyone, but he stared at me by the end. "I thought I would join you today, seeing as I couldn't yesterday."

My face went red as he said this. I was looking into his eyes when a piece of bread hit him on the cheek. We both looked away and saw that Mat had thrown the bread at him.

"Thanks for telling us everything that happened to her." Mat grabbed another piece of bread from Sam's tray and aimed. He didn't even have the chance to throw it. Sam quickly grabbed the bread from his hand. They both started an argument about throwing the bread at Cole.

"So did you hear anything new about her?" I knew that Melanie was talking to both of us, but Cole wasn't answering her. So I shook my head, and she understood.

"They said that she would be out this morning, but she has to stay at home until tomorrow." Cole put his arm over my shoulders and rubbed my arm like he knew that I didn't want to talk about it. Both of the guys stopped arguing and stared.

"Looks like you can't play today. Too bad. I was really looking forward to beating you today, now that I know that I don't have to go easy on you." I twisted around in my chair and saw Rebekah standing behind me with a suspicious smile on her face. It just grew as she realized Cole was here.

"So how come I can't play today?" Her attention was drawn back to me as I spoke.

"We continue playing with the same partners as yesterday." She started to walk away, and I thought of the perfect thing to say.

"Oh, so you'll be petrifying and terrorizing your partner again today. Poor Emma, she doesn't deserve that." She froze in spot again as I talked to her back. She just shrugged and pretended that I'd didn't say anything to her at all.

I looked back at everyone at the table, and they all had their jaws hanging open at me. Except for Cole—he was smiling an encouraging smile at me.

"What?" I looked at them, and they all closed their jaws at the same time, like robots getting the same command at the same time.

"You really don't worry too much of what she can do when you stand up to her." Mat commented me while he got back to his food.

"I don't get why people are so afraid to stand up for themselves with her." I rested my head against Cole's side, and he started rubbing my arm again.

"We all grew up with her, so we know how mean she can be. She's mostly talk, but if you bug her enough, it can get very violent." Melanie explained it to me while everyone ate their lunch.

"She's only nice to the people that hang around her. I should soon be getting into some really bad arguments with her." I looked up to see Cole looking down at me. "She really doesn't like you."

"I'm just surprised that I've survived this long. She didn't like me since she saw me in the hall."

"Isn't that because she saw you talking to her guy?" Mat joined our conversation with a mouthful of food.

"I'm not her guy." Cole stopped rubbing me and stared Mat down with a burning glare.

"Weren't you? Didn't you two date for over two years?" Melanie asked directly to Cole, trying to get him from throwing something harder than bread at Mat. I knew that I wasn't going to be able to contribute to the conversation. I still listened closely, hoping to be able to use it against Rebekah if I had to.

"I broke up with her last year, but she and her followers won't leave us alone. No matter what we try on them, they still come. Now the guys are giving up and letting them follow us." Cole relaxed into the chair and rubbed my arm. I couldn't complain; it was comforting to me.

"I'm just surprised that the new girl comes to town, and she can really stand up to the queen bee of the high school." Sam was done eating, and he held out his hand for a high five. I gave him one, and a smile broke over his face.

"I just don't like being told what to do."

"Give it up for LA. She's about to change our student status for the rest of our high school lives." Mat now held his hand out for me, and I continued to give him a high five. Cole just sat there with his arm around me. Melanie smiled, and everyone continued to eat their lunches.

Gym was way worst than any of my other classes today. Several partners were broken up due to some trips going on, so everyone got assigned partners for today. I got partnered up with Rebekah, of all people.

"This is going to be very interesting." Cole was by my side. Within a minute, he had to go to his assigned court. He gave me a little hug. He left before she walked over.

We didn't say anything to each other for the first game other than calling the birdie, so we didn't want to go near each other. We won three out of four games so far that day.

Coach was very impressed with our teamwork that she gave us time to relax and collect ourselves. She also wanted us to represent the school in a tournament.

"I'm sorry, Coach, but I just simply can't find time in my schedule to practice or even go to it." Rebekah stated with a sweet, truthful voice. I didn't fall for it. I have to admit that she can be very persuasive to the coach. Coach didn't ask us again for our entire break.

While we were waiting to come back into the game, I was watching Cole play his. He was really good. I could tell that was holding back on me the first game we played against each other. *Hopefully, we can rematch.*

We ended up sitting there for the rest of the class. It was a big waste of time, if you ask me. Once the games were over, we had to go over basic things for volleyball.

Cole walked over to me after his game. "See, you survived."

"That's because Coach was watching us the entire time. Rebekah might want to shove the volleyball down my throat tomorrow." Cole started to laugh at my idea, so I lightly hit him on the chest.

"Sorry, but if it looks like she's going to do anything to hurt you, I'll step in. Remember my promise." He then hugged me again, but he didn't smell like the pine trees. He smelled like sweat. I got out of there as fast as I could before I would have any problems breathing.

I got ready in the change room as fast as I could. This way, Rebekah couldn't bug me anymore today. I could also leave and see how was Stephanie's doing sooner.

I was the first girl ready to leave. When I got out of the change room, almost half the guys were already changed and waiting for the final bell to ring. Cole was one of them.

"I thought that you might hurry." He walked over to me, but before he got to me, the bell rang and all the guys left in one big cluster. "So what are you doing tonight?" We were walking to our cars when he said that.

"I was planning to go over to Stephanie's to see how she's doing."

"Want any company just in case it's not that good?" He put his right arm over me again, but he didn't smell like sweat anymore. I was relieved.

"It should be good, if she's just staying home today just to make sure. You said so at lunch. Besides, do you really want to listen to girl talk?" We stopped in the middle of our cars and faced each other.

"Not really, but I can tough it out."

"Don't you have practice?"

"Yeah, I pretty much have practice every night." His face dropped a little as he mentioned practice.

"What team?"

"Teams. I'm on the basketball, hockey, and soccer teams. Most of the teams are almost identical to who's in it." He looked at me, and a smile reappeared on his face. "How many teams were you on in your old school?"

"None. I like sports a lot, but we could never afford to pay for me to play on a team of any sort." I looked around the lot; there was hardly anyone walking to their own cars. Everyone was in huge clusters, just standing around.

"You've changed your money over to the Canadian dollar, right?" I nodded slowly, not knowing where he was going with this. "Well, you would have more money now. It doesn't cost that much to join a team here, plus you would be really good at it."

"I'll think about it. But only after I get caught up in everything else first. Plus I want to get a job soon so I actually have my own money."

"If you want, I can look around for stuff that you might like. I can also ask around for any possible openings anytime soon."

"It's okay. I can do this myself, and you have enough to worry about already. I'm not going to add to it." We hugged again, and we both headed our own way to our cars.

I walked over to my car with my arms warm and tingly from the hug, when a sharp pain stabbed my stomach. The closer I got to my car, the more pain my stomach was in.

When I finally got to my car, a freezing chill went down my spine.

CHAPTER 14

Outfits

I surveyed the parking lot to see if anyone saw me shiver. No one was in obvious sight. Wrapping my arms around me, I continued walking to my side of the car.

When I gazed in to see my warm seat, I saw a piece of paper in my place. I tried to open the door, but it was locked. I quickly unlocked my door, grabbed the note, and sat down in my seat.

Before I opened the note, I checked all the other doors in the car. They were all locked. I ignored the note in my hand and turned on the heat. I was freezing. "It must soon be winter."

After I cranked up the heat, I stared at the note. It was written on the same type of paper as the first one. No one could have gotten into my car though. The only other person that has the key is my mom, and she wouldn't give it to anyone.

I sat in the car, staring at the note for at least five minutes before I realized that I was staring. Placing the note on the seat beside me, I started to drive over to Stephanie's house. I knew that I could always look at the note later.

When I got in the driveway, I debated about bringing the note in with me. Within a few minutes, I shoved the note into my front pocket and headed for the door.

Her parents told me where to go to find her. Apparently, they have a room where you stay if you're sick or injured. They called it the emergency room.

It was the same size as Stephanie's room but not as inviting. The curtains were drawn, with a single strand of sunlight barely getting through. There were three tables with different types of medication spread all over them. The bed was in the middle of the back wall facing the doorway. Stephanie was in the middle of it, typing away on a pink laptop and drinking something, when I walked in.

"Britney! Come sit, and you can tell me what I'd missed in school." She was really perky, which I thought was a good sign. I walked over to the bed and took a seat on the side.

"You didn't miss much. We just read out of the textbook in all the classes I have with you." I made my way to the bed.

"Oh, I already did that. Did the others worry when I wasn't there?" She closed the laptop and scooted over closer to me.

"No, not really. Cole told them mostly everything that happened. Then when I mentioned something that they didn't know, they got mad at him. Mat even threw some bread at Cole for not telling them everything." She looked fine. She had color on her face, and she had lots of energy. *My imagination must be acting up*.

We talked about school for an hour before I ran out of stuff to tell her. We then started to decide what we should wear on Saturday.

"What do you think about dresses?" We were across the hall in Stephanie's closet. It was bigger than my room. When I mentioned that I didn't have anything nice to wear, she sprang from the bed and hauled me over to her room.

"Dresses up here, I think freezing my butt off in a matter of minutes." I was being completely honest with her. I was freezing in jeans, T-shirt, sweater, and jacket.

"Well, how about this?" She was deep within her massive closet, out of my sight. I didn't want to get lost, so I stayed by the entrance.

"I would have to see it to decide." I glanced over to the clock and saw that it was 5:45 p.m. Mom wouldn't be home yet, so I didn't have to worry about being late for supper.

"I'm almost there." It took her another minute to get into view. I timed her.

"How big is your closet?" I looked past her to try to see the back wall to guess how big it was, but I couldn't even see that.

"That doesn't matter. What matters at this point is that we can find perfect outfits for Saturday. Now . . ." She raised both her hands to show me the outfits. "Which one do you like better?"

The first shirt was a small pink tank top with sequins all over in flower patterns. It looked like it wouldn't even meet my pants.

The other one was about two inches longer than the first, thankfully. It was a sky blue tank top with dark navy blue bird patterns. Stephanie started to sway them toward me, waiting for me to say which one I like better than the other.

"Is there a jacket involved with these shirts?" It wasn't that I didn't like them; it was just that I didn't want to freeze anytime soon.

"There is, but I don't know what it will look like exactly, seeing as I don't have it." She started to bounce on the balls of her feet, getting more excited every second.

"So am I supposed to supply the jacket myself?" She shook her head, and I was completely confused. "Explain."

"Cole." Once she said the name, everything clicked into place. She was giving me a tank top so I would freeze, then Cole would give me his jacket to keep warm. "So which one of the shirts do you like better?"

"The blue one, I have a nice navy blue sweater that will go great with it." Stephanie stopped jumping and gave me a firm look.

"No jacket. That way, he'll give you his."

"I said sweater, not jacket. Besides, I'm freezing during the day, so I'll probably be frozen by the time it gets dark." She slowly considered what I just said.

During supper, she kept on whispering "no jacket" under her breath, toward me. Her parents didn't even notice that we were talking during the entire time. I helped Stephanie clear the table, then we retreated back to her room.

It wasn't until we were listening to music when I remembered the note in my pocket. I quickly dug into my pocket, grabbed the note, and told Stephanie exactly where I found it.

"Did you open it yet?" She held the note and was about to open it when she saw me shake my head. She handed the note back to me with an apologetic look on her face. "You should open it."

I took the note from her and stared at it. It was smooth in my hands with rough parts where someone wrote on it. Before I opened it, I took a deep breath and looked up. I saw Stephanie move behind me to see what was written on it.

Soon!

"I have no clue who is writing these and how this one even got it into my car." I looked over my shoulder and saw lines in the middle of Stephanie's forehead as she thought of who it could be.

"We'll figure this out. I don't think Cole wrote either note, but I can't say anything about . . . is it that guy at your house yesterday?" She hopped back around me and jumped down on her bed. The sound of springs filled the air around us.

"It's not Leo. I haven't seen him write anything to know if it was him that wrote the notes." I folded the note and placed it back in my pocket.

"Next time you see him, show him the note and bust him!"

"What happens if it wasn't him?" I wasn't about to accuse someone of something that they might not have even done, at least without thinking of all the possibilities first.

"What's the worst that could happen?"

"Do you really want me to answer that?" I glanced over at her dresser clock and realized that I should go. "I better go, just in case my mom gets home early and panics when I'm not there." I was halfway off the bed when she said something.

"She'll just call Cole, then you two can spend some alone time together for once." I looked over my shoulder where she had an innocent smile spread over her face. "Cole called this morning to find out how I was doing. He then told me everything that happened last night." She shrugged her shoulders like it was nothing.

"I think it's funny how the one day that I have to leave, she comes home and starts to worry like crazy." I walked over to her desk chair and grabbed my shirt before giving Stephanie a good-bye hug.

When I got to my driveway, I was perfectly thawed out. For some reason, it was a lot colder than before. I couldn't park my car in the driveway due to the two vehicles. I think my mom was panicking again, seeing as her car was blocked by Cole's truck.

While I parked on the grass, I reached into the back. I searched for my extra jacket that I stored in my backseat since we moved up here. Better safe than sorry.

I quickly pulled the jacket on as I made my way to the front door. To my surprise, it was unlocked and opened a little. All I had to do was push it, and I got in.

My mom was the first person I saw as I made my way into the house. She was staring at me while I hung my jackets on the coat hook.

"Hey, Mom, you're home early." I ran my hand repeatedly over my arms trying to keep warm as I talked.

"Where were you? I almost headed to the hospital again because you weren't here. I didn't know whether or not you were heading back to LA like you said at the beginning. There are so many things that went through my head that I shouldn't have thought." She started to walk toward me, but then she stopped dead in her tracks.

"Mom, are you okay? I was just visiting Stephanie." I finished closing the space in between us, and she opened her arms for a hug.

"Jeez, Britney, you're freezing." She jumped a little and let go of me. She stared at me for a while. Not saying another single word to me, she headed upstairs. *Hopefully she's heading to bed.*

After she was gone, I headed into the kitchen for something warm to eat. As I walked past the doorway, I saw Cole in his gym uniform asleep on the couch. I didn't have the heart to wake him up, so I just continued on my journey to get warmed up before I did anything else.

I ended up making some hot chocolate for the first time. I followed the instructions perfectly. With my cup in hand, I walked over to view the sleeping Cole.

He was spread out on the couch with his feet hanging over the sides. His head was flat against the cushion with no pillow in sight. He had his jacket and shoes on still as he slept peacefully on his side.

As quietly as I could, I ran to the closet and grabbed a thick blanket from the top shelf. I walked back over to him as I unfolded the blanket in hand. When I got back to him, I softly and smoothly took off his shoes one by one. He fidgeted a little, and when he did, I froze. After a moment, he was still again, and I continued.

When I got done with his shoes, I placed them beside the leg near them. Then I placed the blanket overtop of him. I was almost satisfied with my work when I realized that I forgot one important thing. A pillow for his head.

I didn't know exactly where a spare one would be. I referred to the only place that I knew that had more than one: my room. I didn't know exactly which one would be better for him. I just grabbed the first one I saw that I didn't sleep on. On my way back down, I peeked into my mom's room to see if she was asleep yet or not.

She was, but it looked like she just got to the bed when she finally collapsed. I went into her room and helped her get into bed the right way. As I did, this some papers fell from her front pocket; not knowing what they were, I opened them.

> ***The following letters to your daughter were discontinued. You will no longer be allowed to send her any letters. This is due to the guilt and worry Amanda White is going through. She is worrying about things that should not hold any interest to her. Several times we caught her and some friends skipping their classes trying to watch her sister. If you send anymore letters to her we will discard them right away.***
>
> *Head of Twiddle Academy*

I read the letter several times after, trying to figure it out. She never mentioned that I had a sister, if this was true. *Is this why we moved?* She started to stir in her sleep. I quickly but quietly shoved the papers back into her pocket and returned downstairs.

Cole was still deeply sound asleep on the couch when I returned with a pillow for him. Shaking the note out of my head, I got into position to slide the pillow under his head.

When I placed my hand under his head, he shifted. Not a whole bunch, but enough that my hand was stuck in between his head and the arm of the couch. For a minute, I just tried to move my hand enough to at least try to get the pillow under him instead of my hand.

When I could take advantage of the moment and get the pillow under him, I took it. It wasn't like I didn't like the feel of his hair; I did. It was soft and smooth. I just didn't like the pressure against the arm on my hand. He must have been tired to not bother with a pillow.

When he looked perfectly fine and comfortable, I finished my hot chocolate. It was better than I thought it would be. I even had a second cup before I headed back up to my room for the night. I shut off all the lights downstairs. Thinking better, I kept one light on in the kitchen. Just in case Cole woke up sometime in the night and it was too dark for him to see anything.

Then I went to bed to worry about what my mother wasn't telling me.

CHAPTER 15

Memory

It was the first night since I got here that I didn't have a single dream.

I completely forgot that Cole was here until I walked to the bottom of the stairs and saw him on the couch still fast asleep.

I glanced over to the wall clock and saw that we still had an hour before school started. After I carefully walked over to him, I crouched in front the couch and watched him sleep. While I watched, I tried to figure out a way to wake him up gently. Within a minute, I thought of a perfect way.

Leaving him sleeping, I silently ran over to the kitchen. As quickly and quietly as I could, I scrambled up some eggs and placed them on two plates. Grabbing some forks and ketchup, I walked back to the sleeping Cole. I placed a plate on the table, right in front of his face, so he could easily smell it. It was the nicest thing that I could think of. I knew for a fact that he liked scrambled eggs, so it worked out perfectly.

I sat there eating my eggs while I watched and waited for him to wake up. He shifted a couple times, but he never actually woke up. His eggs were getting cold. When I was finished eating mine, I washed the plate, then I watched him while thinking.

I was running out of time to wake him up. The eggs were proof. He still had to change his clothes. I was going to have to lightly shake him to wake him up.

I crossed the room and sat on the floor, facing him. To my luck, he was facing me. I placed my left hand on his shoulder and started to shake him.

"Cole, Cole, you're going to have to wake up." I talked in a soft voice as I tried to wake him up. He shifted under my hand. A smile broke over my face as I saw that it was slowly working. I continued.

"Cole, there's freshly made scrambled eggs here for you, but they're getting cold." He shifted again, but this time, he moved to the point where his face was pressed against the pillow.

"Hmm, give me five more minutes, Mom." The words were muffled against the pillow, so it took me a while to realize that he thought that he was home and not on my couch. I quickly moved my hand off his shoulder.

"You're not at home, Cole. You fell asleep on the couch." He was shifting again when I said this. He froze in mid-shift. Slowly, he raised his head, and he met my gaze. He couldn't stop rubbing his eyes for a while. He probably thought that this was a dream. That's probably why he called me Mom.

"I'm sorry, Brit. What time is it?" He finally stopped rubbing his eyes. A yawn overpowered him. I got up off the floor, and Cole sat up while he motioned for me to sit beside him.

Before I sat down, I grabbed the plate and handed it to him. "We have about thirty five minutes, if we don't want to be late." He started to devourer his eggs before they got too cold, while I talked.

"I'll just need five minutes to get ready." He talked in between bites, trying to finish the eggs. "I have all my things here with me."

"Shouldn't you get new clothes from your house?" He shook his head while he finished the rest of the eggs. He placed the empty plate back on the table before he turned to me to explain.

"After every practice, a few of us go over to someone's house to watch the game. So every time I have practice, I always bring some clothes for the next day." He leaned back against the pillow with a smart-aleck smile.

"That's smart." He nodded and continued to watch me. "So how come you're here and not over at a friend's house right now?" His smile faded a little when he sat back up. He got closer to me than before. He placed both hands on my shoulders as he studied my face. I could feel the heat coming off of him and felt his warm breath as it washed over my face.

"Your mom got worried when she got home and there was no news from you. She automatically called me on my cell and asked me if I knew where you were. I didn't, so I came over as soon as I could. You really scared us after what happened to Stephanie." I couldn't get over the fact that he said *us*.

"*Us*?" I smiled as I said it, and in return, he smiled back at me. I was extremely glad that I got the smile back on his face.

"Yes, us. You scared me too, Brit. When your mom called, I almost went straight to the hospital." He lowered his hands, and the smile fell completely off his face.

"But you didn't. She probably panicked when there was no trace of me here when she got home."

"Your car wasn't even here. I assumed that you were at Stephanie's." He finally looked back at me, so I nodded, confirming his assumption. "I told your mom, and that kept her from calling the cops. She thought that you were driving back to LA." A corner of his mouth twitched, so I saw that he was fighting the smile now. "She can really worry."

"When I got home, you were asleep, and she was pacing in the hall. After I told her where I was, she went to bed." Then I remembered what I found in her pocket. I didn't want to say anything to Cole, but I would need to talk to someone.

"I'll get changed, and then we can go." He finally lost the battle with the smile. He looked off if he wasn't smiling at me. We both got up from the couch at the same time, but we went our different ways. He headed toward the bathroom with his sports bag in hand. I grabbed the plate and headed to the kitchen.

When I got done washing and putting the dishes away, I just stood there. The only thing going through my mind was the note that I read last night.

I have a sister! I couldn't get that thought out of my head no matter how much I tried. *Why didn't I know about her?* The best explanation I could think of was that I was too young to remember her, and they didn't like to talk about her.

Another thought I couldn't get out of my head was, *Where was she? Is this why we moved?* Mom said that she wanted to get far away from Dad, but what if that was just an excuse? A reason to get me to move away from my life and start over in Canada with her. I remember the day when she told me that we were moving, so perfectly clear at that moment:

It was a normal sunny and hot Friday afternoon in Los Angeles. School was finally over for the day, so everyone was walking to their cars. Except for me and Jessica.

"Come on, Britney, just write your name." My best friend Jessica was standing behind me, encouraging me to write my name on the sports signup sheet. "Come on, Britney, you're not going to leave me alone on the team!" I looked over my shoulder to see her short red hair cover her face.

I didn't even look at the sheet as I wrote my name on it. An enthusiastic smile suddenly appeared, like a cheetah, on her face.

"There, now I'm stuck doing it." Right then, Tarah and Alanna walked up right beside us. When they saw my name on the sheet, both of their jaws fell open far enough to let a bat fly in and out easily.

After she looked at me, Tarah went up to the sheet and wrote her name right underneath mine. She looked over to Alanna, who quickly nodded her head. Then her name appeared underneath Tarah's.

"We have to be there to see you try out. We also have to do this together. Otherwise, it won't be the full experience. We finally have Britney trying out for a team!" Tarah let the stringed pencil fall from her hand, and we all started the walk to our vehicles together. We didn't get far before someone called to us.

"I can't believe that you guys signed up! I was just about to sign myself up. Isn't it so cool that we're all going to be playing roughly on the same team?" We all turned our heads to see Lisa letting go of the pencil.

"Completely cool, Lisa. We'll talk to you later." We continued our way to our cars as fast as we could.

"Movies tonight at my place?" All of our arms were linked together as we walked. I turned my head to look at them while they answered.

It was a tradition that we started when we were little. Every Friday night, we all went over to someone's house and watched movies until we fell asleep in front of the TV. We even get everyone else in their house to leave for several hours. This way we could talk about anything we want, and we didn't have to worry about anyone listening. This week, it was my turn to host and supply the TV for us to use. I love it!

"Of course!" They all almost yelled it at the same time. Then we all laughed about it. We've never missed a single Friday movie night since we started having them.

"I do believe we all know what we need to bring this time." Jessica and Tarah nodded in agreement to Alanna. Everyone contributes to movie night. It all depends on who's supplying the TV. We all have our separate things to bring, but everyone brings movies.

We were at our cars; they were all almost touching each other at the hoods. We said good-bye to each other until tonight.

During my ride home, I had my windows rolled down and my music blaring. I love loud music. The louder and more guitar solos, the better.

Our house wasn't big, but it wasn't small either. We had everything we needed to survive in there. I had my own bathroom, which I really loved. We lived in Mid-City, but it was okay.

When I pulled into the driveway, I had to check the house numbers twice. I recognized my dad's black Ford truck in the driveway. What I didn't recognize was the big moving trailer hooked up to a car that looked like my mom's.

I turned off the engine and walked inside, eyeing the trailer the entire way. Before I even opened the door, I could hear my dad yelling at my mom. *Must be completely drunk for the day, I think it's a record.* I had to take a deep breath before I opened the door.

I was right: my dad was yelling at my mom. After I took a couple of steps inside, I stumbled over some empty folded up boxes. *Boxes?* I grabbed a box and walked to the table. They were in the kitchen, yelling. I was alone in the room. But I could hear them like they were right beside me.

"You d-d-don't have the r-r-right!" My dad's voice boomed, and he stumbled with getting the sentence out right. He was way too drunk so early tonight. Usually, he tells me to drive him to a downtown bar so he could get drunk there. Then later that night, the bartender will call and ask me to come and pick him up. He's been a drunk ever since I was a little kid. Mom always told me that he wasn't like that. When I asked what happened, she just avoided answering me.

"I have the right! Do you really think you'll win when you're drunk before she's even home from school!" My mom's voice wasn't as loud as his, but it was still loud and commanding.

I knew that they were talking about me when my mom said "before she's even home from school." This wasn't going to be good. I'm never in their arguments until it gets too far for them. Then something always breaks. It's usually a glass or bottle. My dad usually broke them.

"S-s-she's not home y-y-yet, so what d-do you think you're doing, starting to p-p-pack for her!" I heard him get up from the table and cross the room to open the fridge. The sound of bottles rattling together filled the air as my mom didn't say anything.

I stood there for a couple of minutes before I heard the door shut close again. I wanted to go to my room. They would never know that I was home. Then I could sneak down the side of the house and enter again after a little while.

The sound of glass breaking cut off my idea and made me run automatically to the kitchen. I had vivid dreams from the beginning where they would break the glass over each other's head and kill them. I didn't want to know if they would actually do it to each other.

When I stepped into the kitchen, the sound of glass cracked under my feet. On the other side of the beer bottle destruction stood both of my parents. They stared into each other's eyes. They didn't even notice me until I started to clean up the broken beer bottle.

"Don't bother, Britney. He needs to learn to clean up after himself for now on." Mom looked at me and started to walk toward me. She took the towel from my hand and threw it in my dad's face. "Might as well start learning how to take care of yourself now." She then took me by the arm and pulled me into the living room.

"Mom, what's going on? Why are there boxes, and why is there that big trailer hooked up to your car?" She pulled me over to the couch and pushed me down to sit, while she stood. She held both of my hands in hers. She bent down closer to me.

"Britney, I need to tell you something that you probably won't like at first, but I believe that you're going to like it after a while of adjusting." Her voice was softer now.

"What are you talking about, Mom?" I stared at her in the eyes, but she wouldn't look at me. It was like she didn't know how to tell me the news.

"I can't live with your father anymore, so the two of us are going to move away from here." Once this sunk into my head, I quickly pulled my hands out of hers.

"Where are we moving to, exactly?" She still didn't look me in the eyes. Instead, she stood up and started to pack some of her books in one of the boxes.

"To a small town in Canada called Silver Stakes. There's a nice small house that I bought for the two of us." I just sat there, frozen as a statue. She just continued to pack as she talked to me. "We're leaving tomorrow morning." I stood up and walked over to her. I placed my hand over the top of the box before she could put the books in. She still didn't look at me.

"Canada! Tomorrow! Are you kidding me! I just got the nerve to sign up for tryouts! I don't want to move!" Right then someone knocked on the door. I looked at the time, but it was early for them to be over already.

"Relax, Britney. I've already packed most of your stuff already." She placed the books back on the shelf and headed toward the door. I went with her. There was a young guy, who was pretty cute, standing in the doorway. He held out his hand, and my mom looked over her shoulder to me. "This man will drive your car to the new house. You're going to have to give him your key so he can drive it." *She really expected me to give my car key to this stranger!*

"Why can't I just drive it?" I knew that I wouldn't win this argument. I hardly ever win the rare argument I had with her. I still had to fight to stay.

"Just give him your key, Britney." She closed her eyes, then she left and went back to packing her books. Withholding the urge to scream at the top of my lungs, I dug into my bag and pulled out my keys. I gave him the key without saying a single word to him. When I was done, I stormed off into my room.

It was after seven before the doorbell rang. I knew who it was going to be this time. Before my mom could tell them about us moving, I ran downstairs and opened the door. Sure enough, it was my friends. They all had their items and had giant smiles on their faces.

When I didn't smile back, their smiles slowly faded, and they started to ask what was wrong.

"Nothing's wrong, I'm just not in a very good mood yet." I tried to convince myself that for the hours that I was in my room waiting for them to come. They always made me feel better about myself.

"Parental fight again?" Jessica took the first steps into the house and gave me a giant hug. "Well, we got the perfect fix for that right here." Tarah and Alanna also gave me a hug while they entered the house. I already felt better, and we didn't even start watching the movies yet.

"Well, we better make this one the best one we've ever had." I didn't want to tell them right then and there. Then everything would be so different during the entire night. When I turned around, I saw that I said that out loud.

The look on their faces told me that I would have to tell them what I meant right away. I headed over to the couch, and they followed. They probably knew that something was wrong when they didn't see my car in the driveway when they came over.

"Apparently, I have to move." Everyone was dead silent. "Apparently, I don't have a choice whether or not I want to. My mom won't leave without me, and she's also packed most of my things already before I even knew." They were still quiet. I knew what little fact I could say to get them to talk. "I'm moving to Canada."

"What!" They all said it at the same time again, and that alone pulled a smile across my face. They then all started to talk at the same time. I just put my head against the back of the couch and closed my eyes. The good part of movie night is that everyone's parents leave the house because they can't stand all of us at one time, especially mine.

Tears started to fall from my eyes as I realized that I would probably never see them again—

"Brit?" Being pulled back out of my memory, I turned around and saw him standing there, watching me.

CHAPTER 16

Silent Torture

Cole was standing in the doorway watching me with worry spread over his face. I felt fresh tears start to fall from my eyes. When he saw that I was crying, he walked over and trapped me against him in a hug. More silent tears left me and dissolved against his shirt.

"What's wrong?" He started to rub my back with his hands. I took a deep breath and was glad that he still smelled like pine trees and not like sweat.

"It's nothing, really." I couldn't talk louder than a whisper. That itself probably ticked him off that it wasn't "nothing." His hands slid up my back to my shoulders. With his hands on my shoulders, he lightly pulled me back so he could see me better.

"It wouldn't be 'nothing' if you start crying all of a sudden. You can tell me anything, you know." He had me, and he knew it. It all depended on how much I wanted to tell him.

"Just missing my friends and everyone else back in LA. I had to leave right away—that, and it's Friday." While I talked, he pulled me closer into him again.

"You can always call them, you know, and at least you made new friends who care a lot about you." He started to rub my back again as he talked to me. I felt a lot better by the time he let me go that everything felt almost like normal.

Except for the fact that this will be the first Friday night I wouldn't have a movie night with my three best friends. No one could replace them, not even Cole and Stephanie.

I stepped away from his embrace then. I mentally shook off the fact that this was going to be the worst night in my life and looked at him. "We better go before we're both late." I looked away from him and toward the clock. We had less than twenty minutes before we would be late.

"Then we better get going." Cole took my hand and led the way outside. He ended up driving me to school, even though I told him that it would be a lot easier for me to drive myself.

I didn't talk much on the way there, just enough to continue a light conversation with Cole. I was too busy wondering how everyone was back home for today. I knew that it wouldn't be the same for them today either; it would be a lot worse. It was going to be a slow night tonight.

When Cole parked in a spot near the back, he told me to stay where I was. I did. After he closed his door, he jogged over to my side and opened it for me.

"Are you sure you're okay, Brit? If you want, we could skip first period." Concern for me was easily displayed on his face as he watched me.

"No, it's okay. You can't miss your first class, and Stephanie's going to be waiting for me anyways." I hopped down from my seat in an instant; pain spread through my legs as I forgot to brace myself for impact. My legs caved, but before I could fall, Cole grabbed my arms and supported me against his body.

He started to laugh as I abashed myself again near him. My face went scarlet red as he reached behind me and grabbed my bag. With my bag in hand, he repositioned me so I was right beside him. His arm was around my waist as we walked to the school. A fair bit of students were already inside, but everyone outside saw us walking together.

My legs were in pain the entire way to class. I was extremely glad that his hand was around my waist to keep me from falling to the ground. There were several more students in the hall than outside who saw us. *Maybe Rebekah will kill me before I have to go through tonight.* I didn't want to be serious about that thought, but I was. I didn't know how I could possibly survive tonight.

Then I remembered that Cole said that I could call them anytime. I made a mental note to call them during lunch. My phone was still set to my old school, so I knew that they had a

PA Day today. We could talk the entire lunch. I just had to decide who to call first.

Cole said that he would see me at lunch, when the warning bell rang loud in the hall. I didn't look at him when I said good-bye to him. I could tell that he was gone when his arm left my waist.

When I walked into the room, I was greeted with seeing Stephanie seated in her chair and watching me. My mood rose a little when I saw her. With a grin growing on my face, I almost ran straight to her. The only thing that held me back was the pain still in my legs as I walked. It was getting better, but it still hurt a lot to just walk.

"See, I told you." Just before I could ask her what she meant, the bell rang, and Mr. Colin started the class. Stephanie just smiled at me and looked toward the front. Mr. Colin pulled a TV setup to the front of the class.

Apparently, every Friday, Mr. Colin brings short clips for the entire class to watch for the entire period. We get to pick which ones we want to watch and in what order.

Why does everyone want to remind me about tonight?

The class dragged on for what felt like forever to me. Whenever I glanced over to Stephanie, I saw the same thing. She was stretched forward in her chair and over the table. I couldn't watch the clips, knowing that I didn't have movie night with my friends tonight.

The last clip that we watched ended up giving us an extra ten minutes of free time at the end of class. Conversations erupted throughout the classroom as the credits started to roll. Stephanie finally relaxed into her chair. She didn't look away from the names displayed on the screen.

"So what did you tell me?" It looked like I pulled her out of a mental thought. Lines formed on her forehead as she tried to think of what I was talking about. I knew she had it when she jumped a little in her seat.

"I told you that you two would be dating by the end of the week." The smile slowly faded when she noticed that I wasn't in the best mood. "What's wrong? It's Friday of all days, so you should be excited. That, and tomorrow, we have the movie date."

"Me and my friends back home always have a movie night every Friday since we were little. We've never missed one except for now." Stephanie shoved her chair closer to me and placed her arm over my shoulder.

"If you want, we could have a movie night." It would be nice to have Stephanie over for a movie night. I debated.

After some mental thought, I had convinced myself of one answer to tell her. I would be completely honest.

"Thanks, Stephanie, but it wouldn't be the same." In my mind, I figured that it would only be the worst thing that could possibly happen. Out of pity, Stephanie comes over to my house tonight to watch movies with me. I didn't need anyone feeling sorry for me.

Stephanie removed her arm from my shoulder, and we started to head for the door. When I stepped out of the classroom, I ran into a person. When I looked up to say sorry, I saw that I ran into Cole.

"What are you doing here?" I wanted to sound nice, but he really was confusing me, standing right here exactly when class ended and I walked out the door.

"I wanted to walk you to class, if that's okay with you. Our classrooms are almost right beside each other, so I thought that I would surprise you." A smile twitched on the corner of his mouth as he held out his hand for me. When I took it, he couldn't stop fighting the smile. Neither could Stephanie; she started to jump on the heels of her feet.

"That's okay with me, and you did. I thought your class was almost halfway across the school." We started to walk toward our next class hand in hand, except for Stephanie.

"It is, but we got an independent when the supply never showed up. So I made sure that I was here in time the bell rang. I walked by a couple of times, but I saw that you were watching a movie." We were almost there, and I didn't want to leave.

"So we'll see you at lunch, I'm guessing." We were at Stephanie's class. She was making sure that we had enough chairs to include him.

"Of course, if you guys can make room for one more." He looked at me at the end, and I nodded. His smile grew. This was my perfect time to tell them what I was planning to do at lunch today.

"I might be a little late today." Stephanie stopped in her tracks and looked at me. "I want to try to call my friends today. They don't have school, so I should be able to get a hold of them." I looked over to Cole, and he had a sweet smile on his face. When I looked over to Stephanie, she was nodding her head like I was an idiot for even mentioning it.

"You should, but you should eat first, then you won't have to worry about it later." I knew Stephanie was right. I nodded, and she made her way into her class. We continued on our walk to ours after we couldn't see her anymore.

We got to my class before we got to his, but we could see the door from where we were standing. He didn't let go of my hand; he held it slightly tighter for a minute. Then the warning bell rang again, and he had to leave.

"I'll see you after class, Brit." He waved to me while walking backward to his class. He didn't take his eyes off of me until he was halfway there. His friend caught up to him and turned him around. *Definitely has balance.* I turned around and made my way into my class.

We actually got to start acting today. When it was my turn though, we had to pack up all the props. Mrs. Wonderlich promised me that my group could go first thing on Monday. They were excited about going first.

I automatically looked for Cole when I left the room. I didn't see him, but I did see Stephanie walking over to me, a smile on her—like usual—as she approached me.

"Where's Cole?" She wasn't even at me when she asked. I didn't even look at her while she asked; instead, I looked around for him.

"He said that he would meet me here." I started to head over to his class. Stephanie was right on my heels as she followed me.

We heard a lower male voice talk to someone who was in there with him. We guessed it was Cole who was being talked to, but we didn't want to walk by and have him see us.

"That's the last time. If this continues again, we're going to have a serious problem on our hands. You were one of my best students in the grade. What happened?" This also helped us guess that it was Cole. While the conversation continued, Stephanie told me some more about Cole's history.

"He was on the honour roll since he was little. Everyone thought big of him." She whispered to me, not trying to let anyone in there hear us. "It all stopped about three years ago. That's when Rebekah started to like him." She looked around, and we started to walk to the cafeteria. Cole knew where we would be. Stephanie continued the story.

"When he found out that she liked him, he started to change. It was little things at first, like not writing down a note. Then it started to escalate." She wasn't whispering anymore, but she tried to keep from other people overhearing our conversation.

"He started to forget about assignments in order to get her attention. When that didn't work that well, he started to skip class. That instantly got her attention. The first time he skipped, he walked right by her class. She saw, and she liked." We were outside the cafeteria, so we stopped. She would have to talk louder in there, and she obviously didn't want anyone else to hear her.

"So did he break up with her, or the other way around?" I was pretty sure I knew the answer, but I still had to ask. He could have just said that when he was the one that got dumped.

"He broke up with her. It was about a year ago. She hates it, so she still tries to get him to ask her out again. She flirts all day with him, and she hangs around him when he's at practice." Stephanie held open the door for me. "You probably want to eat if you still want to call your friends later."

When everyone at the table saw Stephanie, they all stopped and stared. It was like she never left. Cole came in the cafeteria after we sat and started to eat. It wasn't hard for him to join in on our conversation. It was about what Stephanie missed when she was gone for the day.

Melanie informed her on what she missed in her other classes while everyone else ate. Mat commented on several things as Melanie talked. Sam continued his usual routine during lunch. Cole placed his arm around me while he ate. I just tried to figure out who I wanted to call first.

I wanted to call them all, but I wouldn't have that much time to talk to them if I did. I knew that I should call them, but it was hard for me to decide. Hopefully, they would all be together today; and when I call one, I really call them all. But I don't think I have that good kind of luck with me today.

Cole was done with his lunch before me. I wasn't really hungry, so I just ate half of mine. He offered to come with me so I wouldn't be alone. Before I could agree, Stephanie and Melanie both agreed for me at the same time. Then Stephanie said that she would come looking for me when she was done with her lunch.

We slowly headed to the parking lot. It had the best service anywhere around the school. About half of the vehicles were gone as most of the students drive somewhere else to eat.

"I don't know who I should call." We were standing against his truck so I could call my friends. Cole laughed when I said this, so I glared at him. He leaned forward to whisper in my ear.

"Call the person who you were closer with first." He didn't move while I thought about it. It took me a while to think of who that was.

"I guess that would be Jessica. We were all close to each other though." It was completely true. Then when I thought more about it, Jessica and I always did more stuff together than Tarah and Alanna. Cole just stood there watching me hold the phone in hand.

"Then it shouldn't matter who you call first if you're all so close to each other. They would understand." He was still whispering in my ear. I could feel the warmth from his breath on my skin around my ear.

My hands were shaking as I scrolled down my contact list looking for Jessica's cell number. When I found it, I hit "call" and waited.

And waited.

And waited some more, until I heard what I thought I would never hear from her.

CHAPTER 17

Message

"This is Jessica. Leave me a message!" It was her voice mail. I never got it. She always answered her phone when someone calls, even if it's junk.

Annoyed that she didn't answer her phone, I slammed my phone and groaned. Cole saw me, so he waited until I was done before he spoke.

"I take it she doesn't have her phone with her." He backed away from me and leaned against the truck again. He never took his eyes off of me.

"She always has her phone with her. She'd never leave without it, even if she has a date with the most popular guy in school." I rested my head against the truck, remembering how often she's on her phone in a day. "I guess I'll try Tarah's. She has her phone more than Alanna."

I looked at my watch to make sure that I still had time to call her. I dialled the number, and just like Jessica's, I waited.

And waited some more.

"Hey . . . this is Tarah. You know what to do!" Frustration flooded me as I slammed my phone shut again. No one should make it sound like they actually answered the phone.

"Take it she didn't answer?" I looked over to Cole to see him smiling at me. He seemed to be able to melt away my problems when he did that. *I wonder if he knows that.*

"She didn't. I would try Alanna, but she always forgets her phone." Glancing at my watch, I saw that we had about fifteen minutes left of lunch. "I'll try calling them later." I pushed myself away from the truck, and Cole did the same.

"If you want, we could skip the last two periods and do something else. You could try them more often then." At least I knew that he likes to skip often, thanks to Stephanie. But I didn't want to skip at all. Okay, maybe I wanted to skip math. Especially seeing as we had the test today and I never studied. I would never skip gym though. I was looking forward to hopefully forgetting about tonight.

"Tempting, but I still need to know what's going on in math. As you can tell, that's not my best subject." He nodded, and we started to head back to the school doors.

"We could skip, and I could help you out one-on-one." He slid his hand in mine, and for a moment, I actually considered it. Then I remembered that he always skipped with Rebekah. That could never be good.

"Again, I'm tempted, but I doubt that you could help me." His hand tightened on mine so I would look at him.

"Try me, I—" We stopped walking and were facing each other.

"See, I told you I would find you." Stephanie's familiar voice ran down the hall toward us. We both looked over to see her skipping past everyone toward us. "Did you talk to anyone?"

"No, not yet, but I'm not giving up." I was still confused on why they didn't answer me. It wasn't like them. "I'll try again after school." *Hopefully they'll answer me.*

Then it hit me. *Were they avoiding me? Maybe they're acting that I never existed*. I knew that they would have problems today, but at least they had each other to get through it. Would they really make this the worst day of my life by not even answering the phone to talk to me?

"We better get to class." I thought that Stephanie spoke, but then I felt Cole walking away. With my hand being entwined with his, I ended up being pulled along with him. Stephanie was in a state of shock when I looked back at her.

When I waved to her, she waved stiffly back at me. She looked completely shocked that Cole was pulling me to class and not the other way around. I would have watched her longer, but I almost tripped over someone's shoe, so I turned around.

"How about I come over and help you out tonight? I don't have any practice, so I can help you right away." He slowed down and glanced at me. *He must really want to skip math.*

When I didn't say anything on his offer, he continued. "This way, you won't be alone tonight thinking about your friends."

"That's true . . . sure." We walked into class, with our hands still entwined, just as the final bell rang. As we walked to our seats and the class attention was slowly being drawn to the board, I remembered something. "I have to drive Stephanie home today too. She doesn't like having to rush before her brother leaves without her, so I offered—"

"No problem. I'll just drop you off at your house before I drop Stephanie off at hers, then I'll get some tutoring food." Mr. Divident started the class even though half still weren't paying any attention, us included.

I realized why Cole wanted to skip today. It wasn't because he liked to skip; it was due to the fact that after we finished our tests, we played math-related games for the rest of the hour. We started off with playing hangman. I was actually having some fun playing along with everyone. It was a completely new experience from LA.

When the bell rang and signalled the end of class, I was a little disappointed. That was the most fun I've ever had in math. Plus the entire time, Cole didn't let go of my hand until we got to the gym and had to change for volleyball.

I was extremely glad that Stephanie was back today. Now I wouldn't have to deal with Rebekah that much today or have to be her partner like last time.

The girls were changed easily before most of the guys. We had to wait while the coach yelled at them to hurry up. They did, but most of them were wet from the waist up. Coach was not thrilled the slightest about it. As all the soaked guys were running laps, I saw Cole running. He was one of them that were soaked more than the others.

When they were done with their laps, she finally asked them what happened. Max answered for all the wet guys. "The faucet for the shower broke, so water sprayed everywhere. We tried to stop it, but after a couple of minutes, the water stopped coming out." Max stopped his explanation when the coach started to walk to their change room. The guys started to follow her, and most of the girls too, but not all.

I've seen the change room flood before. It wasn't that interesting, but it was really wet. I stayed behind, and Stephanie did the same. Cole walked over to us. When he got close enough, he started to shake his wet hair so the water went on us.

"Hey!" Stephanie and I automatically said in protest to the wetness. Cole just started to laugh silently at himself. We both ran our hands through our hair and over our face to get some of the water out of our hair.

"Okay, Max, get the janitor over here." Coach walked out of the guys' change room with a look of disgust spread over her face. "And try to keep the change room clean from now on." She shook her head and went over to grab the volleyball cart. "Today, we're starting volleyball. Grab a partner, then I'll put you all into teams of six."

Automatically, Stephanie looked over to me with a curious look. When I saw her, I noticed that she thought that I would pick Cole over her. When I looked at Cole, I saw that he wasn't smiling at all. Rebekah was walking over toward him.

"Why don't you partner up with Max, and I'll go with Stephanie." I leaned closer to him so Rebekah wouldn't hear while she walked closer. He looked at me with a smile that grew when he realized that he could do that.

"See, you are smarter than me."

"It's probably only about sports. I stink at actual schoolwork."

"That's why you have me to help you."

"Exactly!" We started to laugh just as Rebekah made it over to us.

"Let me guess—you two are partners, so that means that I'm stuck with you, Stephanie." She only looked at Cole, but he didn't even look at her. He wasn't even looking at me this time. Instead, he was watching the door for Max to walk through.

"Actually, I'm partners with Stephanie." Her gaze slowly left Cole and went to me. Her eyes had a hint of a smile in them that I didn't understand at all.

"And I'm going to be partners with Max when he gets back." Cole still watched the door for him; and when he came through,

Cole started to walk to him, explaining that they were going to be partners again. Max was ecstatic.

It turned out to be a great gym period. I was still on Cole's team while on Stephanie's, so I didn't have to pick between them. I wouldn't know who I would even want to be with more than the other. Rebekah was on another team that was halfway across the gym, so I wouldn't have to play against her for a while.

I was the first server on our team. They voted me because everyone else didn't know how well I actually played, so it would confuse them and make them on their guard.

It worked. After every game, the teams warned each other about my serving and told them to try to keep me away from the ball. The other team never listened, apparently. They all hit and spiked the ball toward me, and everyone on my team let me hit it as much as I could. Whenever I looked at Cole on my right and Stephanie on my left, they always smiled at me, encouraging me on throughout the game.

We were just about to play against the last team when Coach called us all in to explain what we were doing on Monday. Then we had to pack everything up and hit the showers.

"I don't have my car today." I was almost done getting changed. Stephanie was sitting on the bench waiting patiently for me to finish.

"Then how did you get here?" She stared at her watch, checking the time, seeing if she still had time left to catch her brother before he left.

"Cole. I told him that I usually drive you home. He said that he could drive you home today too." I was done changing and was gathering my things together while I talked.

"Good, because my brother would be gone right now." We grabbed our bags and made our escape before Rebekah could come over and annoy us some more this week. "Are you sure that you don't want to have a movie night tonight?"

"Like I said before, it's not the same." I couldn't tell her that Cole was staying over when I told her that I didn't want her to. But it wasn't like he offered to watch movies with me—just help me in math, that's all.

We both were shocked to see that Cole was changed, wet, and waiting for us to come out. He was always the last one out of us to get changed. *He must be in a hurry.*

"It's like he's a whole new person." Stephanie moved closer to me so Cole couldn't hear what she was saying.

"Isn't that a good thing?" She nodded her head slightly, and we dropped the conversation right there.

He entwined my hand with his when I got close enough. He reached over with his other hand to grab my bag, but I wouldn't let him. When he reached over to take my bag, I stretched my arm farther away from him. He let out a couple of sighs as he tried over and over. Every time he tried, Stephanie and I laughed quietly at him. He stopped trying to take my bag when I pulled it over my shoulder and we were outside.

"So are we all still on for tomorrow?" Cole opened the door to the truck, and as Stephanie climbed in the back, he asked us.

"As far as I know about it, we are definitely still on." While I climbed in the front, Cole lightly tossed my bag in the bed of the truck. When he looked back at me, he looked like he was about to jump for joy, ecstatic that we were still planning to go with him.

The entire ride to my house, we talked about some of the movies that were going to be playing there tomorrow night. Stephanie was jumping in her seat as we talked. Halfway to my house, Cole held out his hand for mine. I wouldn't have noticed unless Stephanie nudged my shoulder with her elbow.

Cole had the radio turned down, so we all could easily talk to each other. I was looking out the window while I focused on the music playing, trying to figure out the main notes that they played in the song. I completely blocked out the conversation being held.

The song was halfway over, and I knew all their main notes. I was working on the solo when I was pulled into the present. Cole lightly squeezed my hand to get my attention. Stephanie was leaning over my seat. Her finger and arm were extended. She pointed past the window toward my house. I turned my gaze toward the direction she was pointing to.

My heart stopped when I saw what was in my driveway.

CHAPTER 18

Surprise

There was a black 2003 Lincoln Navigator parked in my driveway. For a moment, I thought that Cole drove up to the wrong place, but then I saw them.

Jessica, Tarah, and Alanna were all walking away from the front door. They weren't used to the weather. They rubbed their hands over their arms, trying to keep warm.

Cole slowed down when he got closer to the driveway. I quickly let go of Cole's hand and jumped out of the truck, leaving him and Stephanie behind in the truck, watching.

They saw me as I slammed the door, and they started to run too. We got to each other in the middle of the road. We were all in a huge hug, with me in the middle of it all.

"We thought that you weren't here. We saw that you called, but we wanted to surprise you." Jessica squeezed me even tighter as she talked.

"We're sorry, but it took a long time to get permission and to plan it all." I didn't know who was talking specifically. I was still in shock that they actually drove all the way up here.

"It's okay—this makes up for not answering my calls." We heard a car horn coming down the street, so we walked over to the side. I looked over to see Cole and Stephanie making their way over. Cole had my bag in his hand as he walked.

"Who's the hottie?" Tarah scanned Cole with her eyes as she spoke. I just rolled my eyes at her and explained.

"That's Cole. We're sort of dating. Beside him is Stephanie. She's one of my best friends here." I knew that I could easily say that if I added the word "here" at the end. It was still completely true.

"You finally get to have some fun in the dating world. If he doesn't work out for you, I can give him a try." Tarah looked over at Cole again.

"I'm sure you could, but I'm not giving him up so fast." She looked at me with her bottom lip sticking out. We all started to laugh at her.

"Cool. Are we still on for movie night?" Jessica linked arms with me and Alanna. Tarah walked over to my other side and linked her arm with me. They started to pull me away right as Cole and Stephanie got to us.

"I take it it's my turn again." We all started to laugh as Cole opened the door with my key. We all entered still linked at the arms. Once we were in, we unlinked ourselves. The three of them made themselves at home. They all went looking for the bathroom and some food.

"Movie night?" Cole was right behind me with my bag in hand. I took it from him and hung it on the hook. He and Stephanie followed.

"Yeah, it's a tradition that we had. By the way, Cole. Tarah, the one with her dirty blonde hair down, thinks you're hot." His confusion left as he considered who I was talking about. Stephanie was right behind him, with a look of abandonment on her face.

"So I take it you want us to leave so you can spend some time with your friends." She started to head for the door, but I grabbed her arm before she could get past me.

"I never said that. All I said before was that it wouldn't be the same without them for movie night. I'm sure they'll be thrilled if you guys stayed. The more the merrier." Just then Jessica stepped off the stairs and was heading for the kitchen. "Right, Jessica?"

She stopped right in her tracks when I said her name. She pivoted on the balls of her feet and headed toward us. A huge smile that said that she didn't have to wait for the bathroom anymore was plastered on her face.

"Yeah, of course." She looked at Cole then turned her gaze to Stephanie before the smile faded as she looked at me. "What did I just agree to, exactly?"

"Having two more people join us for movie night." Then I thought about Cole being here with us. "Of course, only if they want to stay."

Cole met my gaze and nodded to me, taking that I said that just for him.

"Well, they're allowed to stay if they want. But right now, we need some food. The only places we saw coming up were Tim Hortons. After the tenth one, we started to count them. We ended up with about twenty or so." She started to walk backward away from us. I heard a faint growl and realized that they probably didn't eat anything since they left.

"Come on, I think I have some chips that you can snack on while I get something more filling." I walked in between Cole and Stephanie.

Stephanie looked a lot happier that she could stay, but I could see some confusion in her eyes. It was like she was really debating whether or not to stay. As I walked past them, Cole lifted his hand and brushed my arm.

"Why don't I get some takeout? It won't take long to get." Before I could say anything, Jessica answered for me.

"As long as it's something good, do it. I don't care how long it takes." Then she pulled off her sweater. "I knew it was supposed to be cold up here, so why is your house warmer than outside, by a lot?" Stephanie giggled a little under her breath. I think I was the only one who heard.

"Heater—we have it on all the time almost. That way we're not freezing our butts off or wearing a ton of clothes. My mom figured it out one night after we got here. I tried before, but it wasn't that easy." Tarah was coming down the stairs. A look of satisfaction spread all over her face.

"What are we eating tonight, other than the usual?" Before she stopped walking, she made one of her old-time little hops. Jessica and I started laughing. I crossed over to my bag and grabbed $20. With the money in hand, I went and stood in front of Cole.

"This should be enough for some food." I gently placed the money in his hand while watching his reaction to me paying. He didn't say anything about me paying, but he did have a weird look on his face.

"I'll be back in about ten minutes." He placed his hand on my shoulder as he talked.

"Good, that should give us long enough to get everything ready." Jessica walked over beside me and watched us closely. "We brought everything that we were supposed to." I turned my head slightly to look at her.

"Was there any doubt?" I raised my eyebrows at her, and she smiled.

"None, but we might want to get the food out soon. We don't want to start the usual food fighting when he gets back. We all know how that ends up." She looked over at Cole, who was still watching me.

"Okay." I walked around Cole and started to push him toward the door. "You might want to hurry with the food." He planted his feet outside the door.

"Don't worry, Brit. I'll get the food in no time." He turned around, and before he left, he placed the money back in my hand. With a final look at everyone, he closed the door in my face—that way, I couldn't run right after him.

Jessica was right by my side in an instant. I heard Tarah dropping stuff in the kitchen, but I didn't know what Stephanie was doing other than standing there.

"Man, he is cute. If you don't go for him, I'm going to take your place." Jessica was staring at the door while she talked.

"Yeah, and have one of those long-distance relationships. Those always work out in the end." We both stepped away from the door. I needed to see what Tarah was doing in my kitchen, probably before she destroyed something again. Stephanie was leaning against the couch, thinking. I motioned for her to come, but then she just shook her head at me.

"You're right, they never work." Jessica placed a hand on the side of her cheek to think. "Move over, Britney, you just got a new housemate."

"What!" That stopped Tarah in her tracks. She held three giant bowls, two bags of chips, and one bag of party mix in her mouth. When she talked, the bag of mix fell to her feet. "You can't leave us too! What are we going to do? We just lost Britney—now you want to leave us for a guy!" Tarah's eyes started to water. She hated the idea of people leaving her ever since her mother left her when she was two.

"She's not moving in." I walked over to help her with the things. "She's just saying it. She wouldn't want to move up here where there's snow." After I placed the bowls down on the counter, I saw Jessica's eyes almost pop out of their sockets.

"Are you serious? There's snow here?" Both Jessica and Tarah rushed over to the window.

"Not yet, but just think about it. You have to go to school while I might have a snow day." Both of them looked at me with a hateful glare, and then within a second, they smiled and started to laugh.

We finished getting the snacks ready within minutes. When we walked out of the kitchen, we saw Alanna talking with Stephanie. Stephanie still looked like she wasn't sure she wanted to stay though.

Jessica and I were getting the things from the car while everyone else was getting things ready. It took us several trips back and forth before we had everything they needed. When everything was ready, we all sat down on the couch together, waiting for Cole to return.

We were deciding what order we should watch the movies in when Cole finally returned with the food. He was carrying four large containers with three smaller ones in hand. I jumped off the couch and went to help him. The others followed.

Once I had some boxes in my hand, Tarah and Jessica came and took them from me. They then continued to the kitchen while they opened the containers. I was left alone in the hallway with Cole and Stephanie.

"We were waiting for you before we started the movie." He hung his jacket on the rack before he placed his arm over my shoulders.

"I got talking to some guys from the team. Apparently, their planning their own practice for tonight, so they were looking for me." He looked over to me. "I told them that I already made plans, so I was out." I slightly nudged him in the side.

"Why did you do that? You know you should practice with them, and you would have more fun with them anyways." From the corner of my eye, I saw Stephanie start to walk toward her jacket. "Stephanie?"

"Cole, do you mind driving me home?" She walked up to me with her jacket in hand. She gave me a tight hug. "It should be you and them for tonight. It's your tradition, and I don't want to change it." She headed for the door right after she saw Cole nod his head.

"The tradition is already broken. It always starts right after the final bell at school. Besides, it's not like we can continue it, with me being up here and everything." The others came out at that moment, but they went straight to the couch.

"It's okay with me. We still have the movies tomorrow night. You should spend some time with them." She opened the door, and a gust of winter wind came blowing in. Cole put his arms around me to keep me warm. The others turned and started to shiver; they waited for the door to close.

"I'll see you tomorrow, Brit." He pressed me into his chest before he followed Stephanie out the door.

When I turned around, I saw the looks.

CHAPTER 19

Movie Night

"I think Britney got a new nickname along with a new boyfriend." My face went scarlet red as Tarah commented on my life up here.

"Be quiet and start the movie, Tarah." I crossed the room to the empty spot on the couch and fell on the seat.

"Sure thing, *Brit*." Tarah shoved herself off the couch and advanced to the TV.

Jessica handed some of the popcorn over in front of me. I took some, and we started the movies.

We had little conversations throughout the movies, but for once, we were paying attention. Apparently, they've stopped at a rental store on the border, and they bought some new movies just for tonight.

We finished the new movies by 1:00 a.m. At that moment, we refilled our drinks before we continued. Tarah and Alanna both raced to the bathroom while Jessica and I filled the snacks.

"So what's going on tomorrow?" Jessica took some bowls and made her way back to the living room. I followed.

"They have their own movie night up here just for the community. Cole asked me if I would go with him, then he asked me if Stephanie wanted to go to. Now it's a double date, but Stephanie doesn't know who she's going with." Right then, a door upstairs slammed shut, and we could hear Tarah's laughing. We both just shook our heads at the ceiling.

"I'm glad that you found a nice guy, for once." She put the bowls on the table before she started to grab handfuls.

"I've never dated anyone before, so you can't say 'for once.'"

"That's because you were focusing on gym, music, and your parents. Now you don't have to worry about your parents, so it opened up some free space." She munched on her food, knowing that she was right.

"True, but it's not like he asked me to be his girlfriend. He just asked me to the movies on a double date." I grabbed some chips and started to munch on them.

"At least you have a guy interested in you. You should see how some guys act in gym now that you're gone. It's weird. Tarah still wants to do the tryouts, but I'm not sure if I want to." She grabbed the bowl of Skittles and held it as she started to munch on them.

"You should still try out. I know that we did that so we could do something else together, and you guys forced me join. It would still be fun for you guys to continue through with it." I grabbed the next movie and switched it in the player.

"It wouldn't be the same. We wanted to do it together. It won't feel right without you there doing it with us."

"What about that other girl . . . Lisa. She wanted to hang out with us for the longest time." I glanced over my shoulder and saw the questioning look from Jessica. "It wouldn't be that bad—just think of her as the new me in the group."

"Right. No one can replace you, Britney, not even . . . Nope, I can't even think of anyone close enough to replace you."

Hearing a giant thud coming from the stairs, I quickly turned my attention. Tarah was at the bottom of the stairs, smiling.

"I won, but Alanna wasn't really trying."

"Who would?" Jessica and I stated at the same time, showing how often we'd been together.

Once Alanna joined us again, we started the movies. It wasn't long before we were all passed out on the couch, with the movie still playing.

The smell of ocean seawater filled my nostrils as I breathed in the invigorating sea air. I was gazing at a bright blue sky reflecting off of the dark seawater. I was wearing a light green spaghetti-strap dress that went down just below my knees. The sun was beating down on me just like it did back in LA. The silent ocean breeze was playing with my dress as I walked along the beach.

The sun was setting and sending off the most beautiful colors into the sky. It was too beautiful for words to describe. I felt like it wasn't real, that it was just my imagination playing with me, but then I heard her.

It was a sound that was so familiar to me, but I couldn't remember who it was. I turned, and when I did, I didn't see anyone. I looked across the entire beach, but I saw no one. I continued on my walk, but within every three steps that I took, I heard faint footsteps behind me.

This time, I saw a figure in the far distance. I then started to run forward. When I tried to talk, I couldn't find any words to say. I stopped trying to talk and just kept running. Somehow, I ended up running in a raining tropical forest. It was such a change, but when I looked behind me, I saw the beach again.

The forest was dark as night. None of the sunset even entered through the trees. The rain was warm and soft against my skin as I continued to run toward the figure. It was getting closer, so I slowed down.

When I got to them, the rain was pouring so hard. I couldn't see anything other than shapes. It was silent rainfall though. I could easily hear what she was saying.

"I'm always watching, Britney. I'll take care of you no matter what." There was a long pause. I couldn't find my voice again as she continued. "That's what family does." Then right in front of my eyes, she disappeared. "I'll take care of you for as long as I can. Don't ever forget." It was all that she said as she left my sight.

Just as quickly as before, I was back on the beach. My clothes still wet from the rain, dried right before my eyes in the sunset. I didn't know what to say or think to that. I didn't even know who was talking to me. My head was racing. Several minutes passed as I thought about what just happened.

Shaking my head of everything she said to me, I continued my way down the beach. I found a small bonfire lit in the middle of the beach, with no one watching it. Inside the flames, I saw some marshmallows on a stick heating and starting to melt into the fire.

I rushed over and pulled them off before they were completely melted into the fire. A cold hand rested on my bare shoulder from behind me. I jumped away from the touch as I turned around with the sticks in hand.

No one was there.

Drawing another relaxing breath of the seawater air, I tried to gather up my nerves. While I looked into the fire, I swear I saw words. It looked like it said, "*Beware the night.*"

Just to make sure that I was seeing it correctly, I leaned in toward the fiery words. I could feel the heat of the fire heating and illuminating my skin so much. Sweat was staring to form on my face and down my cheeks.

I did see the words, but I also saw something else in it. Not knowing what it was, I moved even closer. I was so close to the flame that I was only inches away from it. All of a sudden, I heard a crackling sound coming from the flame. Right before I could move away, a giant face of a man rose from the flame and came at me.

For once, I didn't sit ramrod straight. I actually jumped right off the couch. It was a good thing that I was leaning on top of Jessica, not the other way around.

I couldn't stand still; I kept on moving from one foot to the other, over and over. Until I saw what time it was. It was 9:30 a.m. I knew that Stephanie would want to spend the day getting ready for tonight. I wasn't sure how early she wanted me over or if she was coming over here. That part wasn't planned.

I spent the next half an hour cleaning up the bowls and the movies. I kept busy so I wouldn't have to think about the dream. I was doing the dishes when Alanna walked into the room.

"Morning. You're up early." She paused in her tracks to give into a yawn. When she was done, she continued her way over to help empty the bowls.

"I couldn't sleep. I got this. Why don't you get your things together? You guys have a long way back home today." I took the empty bowl from her and started to wash it.

"You're right. Hopefully, Tarah lost all her energy for the ride home. She kept on talking the entire time, and when she wasn't talking, she was singing." Alanna shuddered at the memory of Tarah singing.

"I can just imagine it. For everyone's sake, I'm hoping that she's way too tired to even think about singing or talking." We heard her grumble in her sleep, and we started laughing at the idea of her never talking again.

"Are you sure you don't need any help cleaning up?" She handed me another bowl. I took my time cleaning it. *Just need to stay busy.*

"You should get your things together first, then we can go from there. Besides, this gives me something to do." I lifted my head to look out the window as I washed the dishes. Alanna silently went back to the room and started to gather her things.

I could tell that Jessica was up when Alanna whispered for her to get her things together first. They knew that they should leave as soon as possible to beat the weekend rush that would appear at the border.

When I was done with the dishes, I went to check on their progress with their things. Alanna was zipping up Tarah's bag while Jessica was in the bathroom having a shower and brushing her teeth. Tarah's bag was overflowing with items, so I went to help her. I ended up having to sit on the bag while Alanna tried to zip it up. Tarah always packed the most things.

"What are you two doing with my stuff?" We both jumped when we heard Tarah's morning voice behind us. Her hair was all messed and knotted when she lifted her head to look at us.

"We're getting your things together. This way, you're ready to leave when you wake up." I answered in a real relaxing voice. There was no need to get her in a bad mood when she had a long way home ahead of her.

"Okay, wake me up when we're leaving." She turned on the couch and started to go back to sleep again. Leave it to her to sleep the entire Saturday away.

We ignored her when she started to lightly snore and mumble in her sleep again. It took us three tries to close her bag. Jessica had to sit on my lap before we could even get it halfway closed.

When that task was done, we continued to get the rest of the things together. It took us until 11:35 a.m. before we had everything back to normal. I then decided to call Stephanie and see what we were doing for tonight. When I told the others that I was going to call her, they decided to try to get Tarah into the car.

The phone rang three times before someone answered it mid-ring.

"Hello, Mrs. Ozone speaking." Her voice was bright and awake when she spoke. She sounded like she was awake for hours.

"Hi, Mrs. Ozone, is Stephanie around?" I didn't know if my voice sounded as awake as her, but it didn't sound as tired as I felt.

"Yes, she is, just one minute." I heard her walking up the stairs to Stephanie's room. I knew that she was knocking on the door before she opened it.

"Hey, Britney, what's up?" Stephanie sounded just as perky as her mom did. *I wondered how long she's been up.*

"Not much. They're about to leave once they get Tarah in the car, probably. I was just wondering what we were doing before tonight." I glanced out the window and saw them trying to get Tarah into the car. I started to silently giggle to myself.

"Give me about twenty minutes to get everything together, and I'll be over as soon as I can." Before I could ask what she needed to get together, she shut the phone off. Shaking my head in disbelief, I quickly ran outside to help them with Tarah.

CHAPTER 20

Another New Beginning

"That has got to be one of the most excruciating position for a person that I've ever witnessed." I wasn't exaggerating the tiniest bit. Tarah's head was tilted straight back and to the right. The rest of her body was turned to the left, away from any possible chance of the door hitting her when we closed it. She looked so out of place in the car that I thought that she was a dummy. "She'll try to kill you if she wakes up like this."

"That's why we tell her that she went like this after we put her in there." Alanna gave me another hug and headed for the passenger door. "Next time, you're coming back down."

"Sure, if we still want to do it." I closed Tarah's door as carefully as I could. I didn't want to get blamed for her position if I didn't have to.

"Maybe we should make it once a month or something." Jessica trapped me in another embrace before I could say anything. "It's finally your time. Have fun on your double date tonight, for all of us."

"Sure thing. Make sure you answer next time I call though. I might try to call tonight to give you an update." Jessica dropped her arms, and we walked over to the door.

"Anytime—remember that." She hopped in and started the car. The cold was starting to bug them.

"I will. Now you guys better go before she wakes up and starts to yell at us for stalling." I pointed to Tarah, and as I did, she groaned and turned. We all started to laugh.

"Bye, Britney." Jessica and Alanna spoke in between laughs. I shut Jessica's door before they drove out of the driveway.

Just when they were driving down the road, a familiar car came into the driveway. Stephanie quickly got out and came running to me.

"I think I have everything we'll need to get ready for tonight." Stephanie showed her four bags. She shoved two of them in my hand as we walked inside. "Those two bags are for you."

"I already have the shirt, Stephanie. What else do I need?" I opened the one bag slightly to see what was inside.

"I have several options for both of us, and instead of asking you what you had, I just brought mine." When she looked at me, it looked like she was glowing with excitement already.

I closed my bag and kicked the door shut at the same time. Then we started to go to work for tonight.

The entire rest of the day consisted of trying clothes on. We also had to decide what to do with our hair and makeup. We made an early lunch so we would have the entire afternoon to get ready.

"Where are we meeting the guys?" I stepped out of the bathroom in the outfit Stephanie had picked for me. "I'm changing into jeans though." I was wearing the sky blue shirt that I had picked out earlier. I was also wearing a black skirt that went just below the knees.

"Cole said seven, here, and you should wear the skirt." Stephanie changed before me, so I knew that my outfit wasn't the worst one. She had her pink top on along with a skirt that didn't even get to her knees.

"We have about two hours before they come then." I crossed the hall and grabbed a pair of jeans from the drawer to change into.

"That should give us enough time to do our hair." Stephanie started to unwire the wire of a curler, and I got ready for the burning.

To my surprise, it wasn't as bad as I thought it would be. She didn't curl all my hair, just about five or more strands. Then I did the same thing to her. Overall, we were completely done and ready with five minutes to spare.

The doorbell didn't ring until five after. Stephanie told me that they were waiting outside since seven. When I said that we should go, she told me that she wanted to see if they would come up to the door or not. So we waited for them. She was disappointed that only Cole came up.

When I answered the door, Cole was standing there with his one hand on the doorframe, watching me with a growing smile.

"We're ready whenever you two are." I was the one who broke eye contact to look over at Stephanie. She jumped off the couch before she nodded at me.

"We're ready." I grabbed my light jacket off the hanger before Stephanie could reject to it. I was the last one out. With a freshly written letter on the kitchen table for my mom, I locked the door.

Stephanie was surprised when she saw Max in the car. She looked over her shoulder at me quickly before she hopped in the back. Cole helped me in right after Stephanie. Then we started to drive out of town.

Within ten minutes, we were at this parking lot that was already halfway filled with other vehicles. When we got out, the guys went to the back and grabbed several blankets. I figured most of them were for me, seeing as I still wasn't used to the cold winter air.

I started to get goose bumps on my arms before we left the lot. I put my jacket on with shivering arms, and everyone noticed.

"If you get too cold, I can always take you home." Cole placed his arm around me again and started to rub my arm to warm me up.

"That's okay. I'm going to have to get used to it sooner or later." I just kept on looking forward while I walked so no one could tell me that my lips were turning blue.

"Well, you can take your time getting used to it. That's why we brought lots of blankets." From the corner of my eye, I saw Cole shrugging off his jacket. "For now though, I'll give you my jacket. It should be pretty warm by now." I had my arms wrapped around me, so he placed it over my shoulders before he continued to rub my arm again. I could smell the pine forest descending from within his jacket. I then started to take long, deep breaths as often as I could.

We walked for five minutes within some scattered trees before a clearing formed right before us. Several people were seated near trees while they watched some previews on the big, wide movie screen. Even more people were in line at a small concession stand just barely over a hill and in the trees.

Cole led the way to a large pine tree near the far middle of the clearing. Max spread out two blankets and placed them on the ground. Stephanie and I sat close together, and the guys sat on the outside of us. They both placed an arm around us after they placed a blanket over the top of our legs.

"Do you want anything from the concession stand for the first couple of movies?" He whispered in my ear before he asked the others.

"No, I'm good for now. I usually don't start munching until the third movie." I leaned against him as I whispered back to him. He nodded, and then he asked the others. Max wanted some popcorn, and Stephanie wanted some Coke. Cole quickly jumped up and ran over to the stand to get everything.

When he returned, he had their things plus popcorn and a pop with two straws. He handed it to me, so I figured that he got two straws just in case I wanted some.

There were six movies that were planned to play starting at 8:30 p.m. The first three were *Pirates of the Caribbean: Dead Man's Chest, The Creature from the Black Lagoon,* and *Children of the Damned*. I've already seen the first three, but apparently, I was the only one. Thanks to the many hours I've spent actually watching movies.

I was cuddled up into Cole when I got a craving for some caramel-covered popcorn. I easily had enough money to buy some, and it wasn't like I didn't know what was going to happen next in the movie. I've seen it over twenty times because it was Alanna's favourite movie.

"Does anybody want anything from the concession stand?" I looked over and saw that Stephanie was cuddled up with Max. *Well, I think this is going well for them. Both of them look really happy. Or she's just petrified from the movie.*

"No, I think we're good for now." Max answered while Stephanie got too scared and buried her head in his jacket. "I don't want to spill anything on my new jacket." Max had a huge excited grin spread all over his face.

"I can go get it." Cole started to get up, so I put my hand on his shoulder and pushed him back down to the ground.

"No, you don't. It's my turn, and I've seen this movie before, remember?" His hand caught mine, and he slid $20 into our hold. I looked up at him and gave him a hard look, but he just returned with a sweet smile.

"I can at least pay. You still don't have a job, so you need the money for other stuff." I stared at him, but within minutes, I gave up.

"Fine. I'll be back." I got up and let go of Cole's hand.

My hand was still warm from his touch when I got to the concession stand. The smell of fresh buttery popcorn and their freshly made cotton candy filled the air around me. I was right behind two other people, so I had some time to decide exactly what I wanted.

It was $17.50 for large popcorn, a large Coke, and some boxes of candy. I had everything in hand when someone's hand lightly rested on my shoulder. "I got it, Cole. Go ahead and watch the movie so you don't miss the stuff that makes sense." I turned around, and there stood a tall, skinny blond guy wearing all black. He was staring at me like I was the answer to some big important question. "I don't know you." Slowly whispering the sentence, I felt that I knew him from somewhere.

"Britney White?" His dark blue eyes narrowed while he waited for my answer. I didn't know what to say or do; my stomach clenched, and my throat went dry. I tried to figure out what to do. Until then, I just nodded and waited to see what he would say or do next. He gave a quick little nod to himself and looked around slowly. I followed his gaze around and saw that we were completely alone. Not even a person in sight.

"Can I help you with something?" was all that I could manage to say through the dryness in my throat. Even still, it sounded hard, and you could easily tell that I was scared out of my mind. He grabbed my arm in an iron lock and pulled me farther into the darkness of the forest.

"It'll be very quick, as long as you cooperate." He looked over his shoulder to see if anyone saw us, and as he did, I knew that this wasn't going to be good. *Breathe, Britney. Don't let your imagination get away from you now. Nothing bad is going to happen. He probably just wants money; if he does, then he can have it. Breathe and relax.*

His iron grip never loosened. He quickly whipped me around in a semicircle. It knocked the food and drinks out of my hands. My back slammed into the cold bark of a giant evergreen tree.

Quickly, without losing the momentum, he placed his right hand over my mouth to keep me quiet. I could smell and feel the sweat radiating off of him. I didn't want to breathe it in, but my breathing and heartbeat quickened as I watched him.

Staring straight into his eyes, I saw the sclera turn black as the iris and pupil both turned bright gold at the same time.

My breathing quickened even more almost to the point of hyperventilating, and hot, fresh tears started to escape my eyes. *I'm going to die!* A voice in my head kept on repeating over and over to me. He looked around again with his new eyes and breathed a quick sigh of relief.

"I promised her that I would help her out as best I could. You understand why I'm doing this then, right? Family helps family whenever possible. I'm just giving her what she wants." He leaned in even closer to me. "She wants you to stay out of her life forever." He was staring at me, and I couldn't believe what I was hearing. *Rebekah! She's getting someone to kill me! When I hopefully survive this, I'm going to hurt her!*

He widened his mouth, and I saw sharp pointy fangs. *He didn't have those a minute ago.* Then it all clicked in. He was the one that got a hold of my phone number, seeing as he knew where I live. Who knows how many times he's been in my house without me even knowing about it. *He could be the one that made Stephanie get hospitalized.* I've seen a lot of movies about vampires, but like everyone else, I thought it was just a movie and not real. *I'm going to die from loss of blood because of a vampire bite! Just like that other guy!*

He lowered his face closer to my neck, and more tears fell from my face. I didn't want to die—or at least, not yet. I screamed as loud as I could when I felt his hot breath on my tight neck. Nothing happened. I could barely hear it. Just a second later, I felt his fangs caressing the side of my neck. At that moment, instinct and adrenalin took over my body.

My hands turned into fists at my side. They were useless, seeing as I couldn't move them. Just as the fangs stopped moving, my leg jammed into his midsection. He doubled over a little, but that was enough. I quickly twisted to the only opening he gave me. Just as I moved, he grabbed my hand.

My other hand was quick to respond. It formed a hard fist and inserted itself into his nose. He was almost on the ground. A low but growing growl escaped his mouth as he crouched there. I started to run away as fast as I could, but it wasn't fast enough.

He caught me just as I got to the tree barrier of the clearing. I tried to scream for help again, but his hand was fast to cover my mouth. This time, he didn't bother with backing me against a tree. He was too angry.

This time, he threw me to the ground. My breath was knocked out at impact to the cold ground. He fiercely grabbed my arm and turned me over. He was again in my face.

"Now I'm going to make it slow and memorable for me." His voice was harsh and sounded of pure animal. It was mixed with a snarl as he talked. "It will be long and torturous for you, but you obviously want it that way."

Just as his fangs went to my neck again and started to apply pressure, someone knocked into him. His grip on me loosened as he fell sideways. I couldn't move to run. Then a girl grabbed me and pulled me to my feet in an instant.

I looked at the two guys on the ground on top of each other and rolling. The almost-killer was up on the ground, with the other guy's fist injecting itself into his face several times before he pounded other places.

"Breathe, okay? Everything is fine. We got this." The girl put her right arm over my shoulders and rubbed my cold arm. She kept on looking straight ahead, watching the two guys fight each other. She obviously wasn't worried about them killing each other.

"So why are you trying to kill her, Tim?" She didn't speak until they were done with their little fight. *They know each other?*

"Because Rebekah told me that it would help her out a lot if *she*"—he turned his gaze away from her and onto me; as he did, I saw that his eyes were back to normal—"was gone and out of the picture. She says that she's had it with you interfering with what she earned!"

"You should know better than to follow orders from her. You don't even need to talk to her. And you certainly can handle your sister by yourself and not listen to her orders." I recognized the voice, but I couldn't think clearly enough to figure out who it was. "Look at what she has you doing for her now." His eyes never left the lying Tim.

"You're trying to kill my little sister just because Rebekah told you that it would help her out!" She said the words, but I didn't believe her. I was an only child since birth. *She must just be saying this to get him to leave me alone.* But then I slowly remembered what the letter said.

"This isn't the way, Tim. Don't make me hurt you even more." As the guy said this, he got off of Tim and turned toward me. When he did, I finally saw who had saved me. Leo. Leo started to walk toward me, when he suddenly stopped. "Amanda, she doesn't look so good. Maybe we should take her to the hospital?"

"No, I can't! Mom will find out. She's way too busy with work to deal with all the paperwork." Everything started to go fuzzy when I started talking, and parts of my body were going numb again. Amanda continued to rub my arm, probably trying to keep me up and awake.

"It's okay, Britney, you'll be perfectly fine. We southern girls are a lot tougher than northern. She can handle it." I looked up at her, and she had a victory smile spread on her face. I looked around and saw that Tim had bolted after Leo got off of him. I didn't even hear him get up and leave.

"Where did *Tim* go?" I looked around, but all I could see was fuzzy darkness in front of me.

"He went back to the school. He probably won't tell anyone about this, but he will have some marks by tomorrow. I guess it's our decision whether or not to report him if he creates a story of how he got them." Leo walked closer to me, but it didn't make my vision of him any better. It went worse. Before, I could see colors; but now I just saw colourless moving shapes.

"Well, if we don't, he could just try to kill her again later. I'm not willing to lose my sister again for good." Her arm got sturdier against me. It wasn't long before I was leaning against her for a moment.

"I'm not your sister. I have no sister. I'm an only child." I quickly straightened up and tried to get out of her arm.

Things were starting to sway when I talked, so I tried to say as little as I could. I couldn't even think straight. A strong part of me wanted to accept it. I was used to the idea of being by myself. I was afraid of having someone close to me that way.

"Maybe she's changing? She looked like she was pretty shaken by all of this." Leo took another step toward me. His hand was extended to me in a gesture of help. He could probably tell that I wasn't myself at the moment.

"No, only the opposite gender or twins. Otherwise, it's only one kid from a family that goes through the change, remember? She's just overwhelmed by everything. She just learned that she has an older sister, for one." I tried to listen, but everything was getting all mumbled up in my head. It took me a while to figure out what she said. When I looked at her, I saw that she changed.

There was no smile on her. She was clearly concerned and worried about me. She took another step toward me also. She looked like she was about to panic if something else happened to me tonight.

"I gotta get back. They'll be wondering where I am." I turned away from them and took a couple of steps toward the clearing or at least in the general area. *Cole or Stephanie will see me and help me.* After my fourth step, everything went black, and there were no noises as I fell to the ground unconscious.